Never give up your dreams.

THE LOVES OF MARIE LAVEAU

A HISTORICAL FICTION NOVEL

by

Dolores Else

Also by Dolores Else

The Women of Burgundy Street

The Amulet

Glossary

banns: public announcements of a proposed marriage in the Catholic Church

bonne nuit: good night

café au lait: coffee with milk

creole: mixed, either black and French, black and Spanish or French and Spanish

etoufee: a stew

fete: a party or used as a verb, to pay high honor to

gens de couleur libres: free people of color

gris-gris: a voodoo charm or amulet

marchande: one who sells foodstuffs or merchandise

lagniappe: something a little extra

les vendeuses: the sellers

metis: people of mixed race

mon Dieu: my God

pain perdu: what Anglos know as French toast

piaster: Spanish coin

place: a woman who enters into placage

placage: legal contractual agreement between a man and woman without benefit of marriage, often between a white creole man and quadroon or octoroon woman

rue: street

s'il vou plait: please, if you please

tignon: required head wrap worn by slaves and women of color

Vieux Carre: The Old Square known today as the French Quarter

Chapter 1

It was nighttime, her favorite time of day when she'd meet her lover. Her mother would doze off in her rocking chair, and Marie would creep out of the cottage like a thief in the night. When she'd return, she would walk her mother to her bed, and Marguerite would never know she had been gone.

Marie walked up the *Rue* Saint Anne to a place with a grassy knoll near the levee along the Mississippi River where they usually met to make love. This young creole girl could have passed for a beautiful Spanish lady with her light skin and dark, sparkling eyes until you looked up to the tignon she was required to wear on her head.

She watched the ships in the harbor swaying gently in the current and waited with an impassioned heart. When she saw him walking toward her in the distance, her excitement made her tremble. She called his name in a muffled voice. How these visits with him made her life happier! It was almost like her father's visits to her mother, except that her father would return to his wife, and Marie wanted to be Jedidiah's wife. He welcomed her with arms outstretched, and they held each other in a long embrace.

"I was worried you wouldn't come tonight," she said.

"Oh, I had to see you. But I can't stay long."

"You can stay for a little while with me, can't you?" Her wistful eyes looked back at him. She did not understand his rush.

They lay on the bruised grass, arms around each other. The cool night air was full of summer sounds. Cicadas and crickets whirled about.

He looked into her dark, shiny eyes. "I'm leaving to go up north for work with my family."

"You've never mentioned leaving before." A shadow fell across her sad face as she tried to understand that he was leaving her.

"I'm sorry, Marie, but I must go. My mother and brothers are packing the wagon to leave at daybreak. My father is fixing a broken wheel and sent me for a part. I only came to tell you I have to leave, but I'll come back for you as soon as I can, and we'll be married. If I don't get back to my father soon, he'll take a strap to me." He wrapped his arms around her, kissing her warmly, got up, and immediately sped.

"I'm going to have your baby."

The words poured from her mouth, escaping into the wind, swooshing between the crackling leaves in the trees. She stood up and watched him running, as tears stung her eyes. She stared almost not believing the sight of him growing smaller and smaller. He never looked back.

Chapter 2

"Oh, *Maman*! The pain! The pain!"

Marguerite was never known to be sympathetic, not even to her children. "Yes, Marie. I do see you have pain."

"*Maman*, help me. Please!"

"Daughter, you have just begun your labor. You have a long way to go before I call for the midwife."

"Can you give me something? Please!" Marie's sixteen-year-old pleading eyes begged her mother for some miraculous relief."

"Do you think if that boy was here, he would do anything for you? You silly girl. Getting into trouble with a boy who has nothing. Nothing! What is this boy's name?"

"Jed. And he loves me."

"Ha! How is he going to take care of you and your baby?" Marguerite looked down at her daughter accusingly, a sudden thought reaching her mind. "What kind of name is that?"

"Jedidiah. I call him Jed. We are going to be married."

"Oh, you foolish child. Married? Well, where is he now?"

"He's gone up north for work to make money for us."

"And you believe this young boy who has nothing?" she yelled.

"Oh, *Maman,* the pain is worse." Marie hunched over and clutched herself.

"You'll suffer more than this labor pain if you keep believing that young boy will take care of you. You could have had a protector, Marie, a man with money who would take care of you and your child. That boy of yours is never coming back to marry you. But no. You're so stubborn."

"Maman, don't keep telling me that. I believe he's coming back."

"You believe. Nonsense. You silly, silly girl."

"Oh, why are you torturing me like this? I'm suffering. Please go and get Martha."

⚜

"Please, leave us, Marguerite. I want to calm Marie." Martha flitted her fingers up toward the door. "Now, just relax, Marie. Breathe slowly. Think about the little baby you're going to have today."

"Oh, Martha. I'm so happy you're here. The pain is so bad."

"I know, *chere.* Here, bite on this rag when you must."

Marie bit down hard on the cloth and grunted from the pit of her stomach and screeched from within.

"Okay, now, it passed, didn't it? The pain?"

Marie let out a hot breath and nodded.

"Now, try to sit up. Come on." Martha braced Marie to a sitting position. She took a jug from her basket and poured herbal tea into a cup. "Here *chere,* sip this."

Marie shook her head and shrunk down.

"Come, come, *chere,* it will help you." Martha forced the tea to her lips as Marie let it dribble down her chin. "You must try, Marie, or we'll be here for days. This will shorten your labor."

Marie slurped noisily and lay down.

"Just rest. I will check to see how far along you are. Don't panic. I won't hurt you." Martha placed her fingers across the birth canal. "You have a little more ways to go, *chere.* "

Marie screamed in pain.

Martha sang to Marie and continued to give her sips of tea for hours. When the labor pains were in their final hour, Marie begged God to take her. "Take me, God. Please!"

"Bite hard. Bite hard, Marie. Here take my hands. Push me hard!" Martha yelled. She checked to see how far along Marie was in labor. "I see you are close. Just bear down."

"I can't. I can't, damn you, damn woman!"

"Come on, little girl. Push me! Slap me if you have to."

Marie's face contorted as she pushed with a look of horror, her body trembling in agony.

"One more push," Martha urged.

"No! I can't."

"I see your little baby's head peeping through. I see him. Let him come into this world."

Marie moaned with one last push as the baby's head came through.

"Oh, he's coming, Marie. He's coming!"

As the baby presented herself to the world, Martha pulled out her knife and cut the rubbery chord, pulled the infant off the bed, and wrapped her in a towel. "Oh," she laughed in surprise.

Marie peered up. "What is it?"

"It's a little girl," Martha said.

For the first time, a smile peeked through tears rolling down Marie's cheeks, and Martha saw relief in Marie's face. "You're very lucky, Marie. She looks good. Yes, I'd say this is a good baby." She wiped the baby clean and handed her to her mother.

Marie looked at her infant with love. She touched the child's fingers one by one and opened the towel to examine the tiny body. Momentarily, she forgot the stagnant air in the room and the grueling pain she had felt in her abdomen and the lonely nights waiting for and longing for Jed to come home to get her. The suffering went away for a wonderful moment when her full attention was on her beautiful child. Her fingertips touched the soft skin of her baby and she marveled at her beauty. And now, her thoughts took her back to loneliness without him, and she kept seeing him running away from her on that last night that they were together.

Martha gazed at the tender love scene and suddenly saw Marie's face go pale, tears exploding from her eyes.

"What's the matter?"

Marie looked up at Martha shamefaced. "I'm sorry I yelled at you."

Martha slapped her palm in the air. "Don't fret over that. I always get that from my mothers."

"*Maman* says that Jed will not come back to marry me. Do you think he won't come back?"

Martha noticed her hurtful expression return. "Of course, he'll come back for you and your child. Don't worry so. You are a mother now. Just think of your child."

"But he doesn't know he has a child. He may never come back," Marie cried.

Chapter 3

Marie fawned over her little daughter constantly much to the chagrin of Marguerite. She carried her everywhere she went.

Marie had planned to see her neighbor who promised to teach her the intricacies of hairdressing. Little Felicite had fallen asleep in her arms, and Marie decided to leave her sleeping in her basket. "*Maman,* will you keep an eye on Felicite? She's sleeping. I'm going to Dehlia's to show me how to better tie those rags around the hair."

"Yes, go. You need some time away from her," Marguerite called out.

Upon returning home, Marie immediately went to her nine-month-old child and picked her up from her basket. The child felt cold and lifeless. Not believing what she felt, she rubbed her little arms and legs but felt no life, no sound. *"Maman,* come quick!"

Marguerite appeared and witnessed her daughter's shock.

"*Maman*. What does this mean? She will not utter a sound or look at me. What does this mean? It can't mean…. Did you hear her crying when I was away?"

"No. She slept the whole time."

Marie cried in agony, wailing. She ran from the house to her confessor, Father Antoine, while clutching her child. She banged on his door in hysteria.

The Spanish monk dressed in his brown robe with the hood draped on his back and a heavy, white rope around his waist appeared calm, motioning for her to come in. "What is it, my child?" His gray beard from the top of his chin to his neck bobbed as he spoke.

"Father. Look! My baby. Has God taken her away from me? My mother says that God has punished me for having this child with someone who can't take care of us."

Father Antoine gave Marie the sympathy she never received from her mother with an embrace. "My child, God does not punish us in this way. God forgives us everything."

"Then, my mother is wrong?"

"Sit with your child here. Yes, she is wrong in saying that God is punishing you. God does not work that way. But don't blame your mother. She does not know any better. Perhaps, she was taught that by her mother or a teacher who did not know any better. We will pray for them."

"My mother wants me to enter into placage. I want to enter into Holy Matrimony with a man that I love."

"I'm so happy that you want to marry in the church. The Ursuline Sisters have taught you well, Marie."

"Yes, they have taught me all of my prayers and The Commandments." Marie nodded with the first half-smile.

"Don't be too hard on the others who were not as fortunate as you who were not taught by the Ursuline Sisters. The placees have not been educated like you. They are victims of their circumstances. We should not judge them."

"Yes, *Pere,* my mother repeated your Sunday sermon to me and told me placage is not a sin. She says Pere Antoine approves of it, so why is it not good enough for you?"

Pere Antoine closed his eyes. "I hope I have not misled my people. Many have criticized me for telling my parishioners not to judge the placees, and for baptizing the children of the placees. It is not that I approve of that state of living with a man outside of matrimony, but I believe that Jesus would not condemn them for their upbringing and circumstances."

He took the child from Marie's arms and looked into Felicite's closed eyes. "We don't understand why innocent children die in their sleep. I pray that your little soul will be given eternal life by Our Lord Jesus Christ through His Divine Mercy in the name of the Father and of the Son and of the Holy Spirit."

He sat next to Marie, and they prayed together. "Your child has been baptized and prayed over, and is now in heaven. She will wait for you for when you go to her. Pray for your mother and all who offend you. Marie, you must try to be busy so that your mind does not dwell on your sorrow. Come with me next week to the prison and pray with the prisoners. Take them some food if you can. Can you do that, Marie?"

"Yes, Father, I will try."

"Good. We will have a funeral service for little Felicite here on Saturday. And it will be a blessed day for the family."

Her face lost all its gentleness, as if the sun had suddenly gone behind a cloud. Marie drifted through the house day and night like a sleepwalker, eyes wide but not seeing. The life that was in her body had left her and now had left the world. She did not see or hear but mourned in her own way, not crying but occasionally wailing out to her child. "Felicite! Felicite!"

Chapter 4

Marie was beginning to believe that Jedidiah might never come back for her. Marguerite insisted that she go to the quadroon ball to find a man who could take care of her and enter into placage. Marie hated the idea of having a man take care of her. She now had some rich, white, hairdressing patrons and felt she could take care of herself.

Many free mulatto and quadroon girls, like Marie, attended the quadroon balls, looking for security. Marguerite delighted in the idea that her daughter would meet a rich white planter and provide her with a home and security for children she might have with him. Marguerite never had a marriage or a contract of placage. She was the mistress of a quadroon man who had a rich wife and family and never provided her with a home. She envied the placees who had homes provided for them and a promise of education for their children. Fortunately, Marguerite had a home that her grandmother, Catherine Henry, a marchande, had purchased. Many free colored women during this time were property owners and business people themselves. Marie saw no reason to look for a man to give her property.

Marguerite had Dehlia sew Marie a beautiful, red ball gown with matching tignon. She half-convinced Marie to attend a quadroon ball. Marie's red gown contrasted greatly against her light skin.

"Now stand straight, Marie, while I pin this in the back.

Oh, you look stunning in this." Dehlia knelt to pin the back of Marie's waist.

Marie could not hide her disposition. "This is a waste of time."

"Bah! You'll see how much better things will be for you when you meet the right man," Marguerite said.

"The right man? One who is married and probably already has children?"

"Yes, and one who could provide you with things your Jed never could."

"Maman, please don't make me go." Marie's charismatic voice and insistence almost made her mother give in to her.

Dehlia tried to make peace. "You look absolutely ravishing in this ball gown, Marie. Doesn't she look ravishing?" She turned to Marguerite. "And what man in his right mind could ever resist your beautiful daughter?"

"I know. Tell her, Dehlia, how things will turn out right for her when she meets the right man."

"Now, you go and have a good time, Marie. I'm sure every man at the ball will have eyes for you. You will have your pick." Dehlia stood back and admired Marie.

Marie and Marguerite walked the steps to the second floor quadroon ballroom with Marie aiding her mother. Only white men and free women of color were allowed to attend with their mothers or protectors.

A young woman greeted them with an infectious smile. *"Soyez le bienvenu!* So happy that you could make the ball."

"Thank you, child." Marguerite greeted happily. She eyed her daughter and bit her bottom lip, as she noticed Marie's unhappy mood.

Marie had a curl lay before each ear, her hair piled high on her head covered with a red tignon with green threads running through in seven points. She made her entrance in her red gown, gracing her body with every step she made in her rhythmic walk, her mother walking proudly beside her. They entered the wide hall with lit sconces holding gas lamps lining the walls and music already serenading them. Seating was scattered on both sides with turbaned mothers, some dark, some light, with their young, mostly fourteen and fifteen year old daughters who had crushed red rose petals applied to their pale lips. Mothers and daughters took their places and waited, eager to enter into a contract of placage with one of the creole men standing. Some of the men were single, some married, but all were rich.

For the most part, it was orderly and elegant. It was rare that a brawl started, but when it did, the mothers would take their daughters home in carriages waiting outside for them.

Next door housed the Theatre d'Orleans where the gentlemen went to the theatre with their wives and slipped into the Quadroon Ball to look across at the pretty bronzy faces of fourteen year old girls eager to meet a generous creole man. If a creole fancied a young girl sitting with her mother, he would ask for a dance and meet the mother. Often, he would negotiate with the mother for placage with a young girl of his fancy.

"Now be polite, Marie. You look like you're pouting. Don't pout," Marguerite said. "Smile!"

Marie fanned herself, not noticing the men looking her way.

A short, balding Creole dressed in tailcoat approached with an eager smile. He looked at Marguerite. "May I have the honor of dancing with your beautiful daughter?"

She could feel her heart swelling, elated at such an early invitation. "Yes, m'sieur. I'm sure she'd be delighted to dance with you."

Marie snapped her fan shut and rose without a word or a smile and walked to the dance floor.

The old cypress dance floor seemed to dip a bit as the dancers waltzed past Marguerite. She thought she felt a pleasant breeze as the placees-to-be danced around the ballroom with smiles they didn't feel, showing white teeth against their light brown complexions. The candle-lit chandeliers glowed against the light bronze skin of the quadroon waltzers, as they passed. Marguerite's heart skipped a beat as she watched her daughter dance, wishing for a match with a rich Creole.

"Your gown is most exquisite, mademoiselle. And to go with your most elegant beauty." He raised his bushy eyebrows to make his point.

"Thank you," Marie replied.

He looked into her dark, luminous eyes. "Have you been to a quadroon ball before?"

"No, this is my first time. With my mother always being ill, and I'm the only caregiver, I'm not able to get out."

"Oh, your mother has an illness? I'm very sorry."

"Yes, and she will always have to live with me because I am all she has. She never sleeps a whole night, and she insists on sleeping in the same bed with me. I never get a whole night's rest."

"What is your mother's illness?"

"She has many. Her heart, her arthritis, and her stomach. Oh, her stomach is the worst." Marie furrowed her brow and shook her head in dismay. "She loses her food all the time. During the night, it usually happens. The vomiting. That's why I never get a full night's sleep."

"I'm very sorry to hear that." His smile left his face replaced with repugnance. He paled at her words, eager to take her back to her mother after they danced.

Marie saw his nose rise in a wrinkle as if he smelled the vomit.

"Thank you for the honor, mademoiselle." He trotted off in haste.

Marguerite looked after the man who seemed to rush off in a hurry. "I didn't even get to talk to him. Why didn't he stay to find out more about us?"

Marie shrugged her shoulders. She noticed a rather plain looking girl in a gray ball gown sitting against the wall alone. Walking over to her, Marie started a conversation. "Are you here alone, mademoiselle?"

"No, my mother is over there," she said, pointing to a matronly looking woman talking to a man bent in conversation. "She thinks she is a great negotiator, but she hasn't been successful in procuring a contract."

A young, handsome man walked up to them, eyeing Marie. "Mademoiselle, would you do me the honor of dancing with me?"

Marie put her hand behind the girl's back and pushed her up to a standing position. "My friend would be most delighted," Marie said with a smile.

The man, not wanting to slight the young woman as she stood, escorted her to the dance floor like a perfect gentleman. The mother looked back at her daughter on the dance floor and smiled.

When Marie returned to her mother, Marguerite asked, "Why aren't you dancing and why did he choose her?"

"Can't you see? The men don't want beautiful girls who might be stolen away from them when they're not with them.

They want plain looking girls who will be there when they want them."

"What are you talking about? I never heard…"

"Are you blind? Look who he's dancing with?"

Marguerite looked confused. "What? Why I…"

"I don't have a chance here. I'm leaving." Marie turned and walked toward the exit. She ignored the admiring glances of the men as she passed them, walking through the French doors to the exit and down the stairs.

Marguerite looked stunned for a moment and then rushed to follow her daughter. She did not hear the voices raised in farewells or invitations to meet again, as she had anticipated if they had stayed to the end. She heard the usual laughs and witnessed coquetting under satin masks as she walked hastily by and knew there would be no flirting or roving eyes toward her daughter tonight. She stopped for a second and listened to the wafting ballroom music before retreating through the French doors. She clopped down the wooden stairs, following her distraught daughter. "Marie, wait for me."

Chapter 5

Marie still heard her baby's cries in the night and would wake and run to her basket. As she grieved for her child, she took Father Antoine's advice, working hard to dissuade her loneliness and did many good works.

She gained more patrons in her hairdressing business, and also visited the prisoners weekly with Father Antoine. Many people watched the prisoners hang in the gallows, but Marie did not watch the hangings. She left after she prayed with them.

Dehlia indulged Marie her slave, Manvil. At times, Manvil would help Marie plant her garden, and Marie, in turn, would give Dehlia vegetables and fruit from her trees.

Marie allowed the Choctaw Indian women who sold herbs in town to camp on her yard. They started to plant indigenous herbs in her garden and taught her about their remedies. She also had learned from her mother and grandmother and became expert in the field of herbs.

As Marie walked the street toward Madame Hebert's Garden District mansion, she loathed the lavish homes, thinking it vulgar to have front doors and gardens open to the streets with no privacy walls in front of the homes as the homes in the Vieux Carre. *They live like fish in a fish bowl with their front doors on view to the world.*

A mulatto butler opened the door for Marie and led her up the winding staircase to Madame Hebert's boudoir. "Good morning, Madame Hebert. I trust you are well this fine morning."

"Mawree! I'm so happy to see you," Madame Hebert said, sitting at her dressing table.

"I see you are well prepared for me, Madame." She eyed the table with a large basin and two huge pitchers of water. Bars of lavender soap sat beside the basin on top of bath cloths. Marie set her burlap bag on the floor.

"Yes, shall we get started? We can discuss the way I want my hair styled after you wash it. I can't wait for you to massage my scalp. It feels so ravishing the way you do it, Marie."

"As Marie massaged Madame Hebert's scalp, madame asked Marie, "Do you like to dance, Marie?"

"Yes, madame, I love to dance."

"I remember when Friedrich used to take me dancing. It was so lovely. Those were the best times of my life. But he doesn't take me dancing any more. He disappears on Saturday evenings, and I never know where he goes. Maybe to the cockfights, but

I'm not quite sure. And sometimes he disappears at the oddest times without explanation."

Marie gently towel-dried madame's hair and noticed the sadness in her eyes when she looked at her reflection in the looking glass.

"Are you sad?" Marie asked.

"Yes, I must admit I feel down. I don't understand what's going on in my own home." Madame Hebert quickly burst into tears and then immediately wiped them dry and opened her eyes wide. "He never takes me dancing any more. He never holds me either like he used to. No one could ever know how much I miss that. I feel so alone on Saturday nights when he goes to God knows where."

"I believe that will change for you, madame."

"How do you know?"

"I feel it in the stars. The spirits are telling me that your life will change and you will be happy. I even see monsieur taking you dancing."

"How can you possibly see that?" Madame looked up at Marie, waiting for an answer.

"The spirits let me know about you," Marie said.

Almost finished with wrapping Madame Hebert's hair around strips of rags, Monsieur Hebert bounded into the room carrying their sick daughter, Dorotea, in his arms. "She is hot!" he declared.

As the five-year-old child was brought to her mother, Madame Hebert felt her feverish daughter's forehead and arms. *"Mon Dieu!* The child is really in great fever!"

Dorotea's eyes did not open to her mother's voice.

"We must take her to her room and cool her down," Marie advised. Monsieur Hebert carried the child to her bed with the women following. "Can you get your servants to bring cold rags as cold as they can get them and bring them?"

Monsieur Hebert left the room, beckoning to his servants.

"Oh, my child. I had no idea you were this sick," Madame Hebert wailed. She looked to Marie for some comfort.

"We will cool her down. Don't worry, madame."

Monsieur Hebert appeared with servants carrying cold rags.

Marie immediately pressed the compresses on the child's face and neck and traveled down her body.

Dorotea screamed and squirmed from the coldness on her hot body.

"There now. You will be okay." Marie soothed Dorotea, speaking softly and stroking her head. "We will make you well."

"What else can we do for her?" monsieur asked.

"I have herbs for a fever. They are at my home in the Vieux Carre. I must leave right now. It will take me time to walk home."

Madame Hebert turned to her husband. "The word is, Friedrich, that Marie is very good with herbs."

"You needn't walk, Marie. I will take you in my carriage. Follow me," Monsieur Hebert urged.

❧

Marie ran into her home as Monsieur Hebert waited. She put the herbs that the Choctaw women had given her into a small, cloth bag. She ran next door to Dehlia's house. "Dehlia, I have to have Manvil help me. I'm going to the American side to help a young girl with the fever. Her father, who is the Chief of Police, is waiting for me in his carriage."

"Manvil, you go with Marie. Do as she says," Dehlia said.

"Yes, mam'zell." Manvil stood straight and tall with a smile on his black face, happy to be of service to Marie.

Before they left Dehlia's home, Marie looked Manvil straight in the eye. "Now, Manvil, we're going to go into the kitchen at the American's house. You make friends with the servants. They are nice, like you. Find out what you can about the family and where the husband goes on Saturday nights and if he drives himself or does a servant drive him. We are going in Monsieur Hebert's carriage. Remember what his carriage looks like. Will you remember that?"

"Yes, mam'zell. I will remember everything and tell you."

Marie and Manvil hurried to the carriage. "I must take my slave, Manvil, with me to help me carry the pots and strain the teas," Marie explained. *As if I can't strain tea by myself, hmph!*

"Very well," Monsieur Hebert agreed.

When they arrived at the Hebert residence, Marie explained that she must make the tea herself. "When the fever is this high, I want to make sure I get the right dosage and make it myself."

"I understand," Monsieur Hebert said.

"Go and do what I told you to do," Marie told Manvil as they entered the kitchen. She made the herbal tea and proceeded to Dorotea's boudoir.

Manvil became acquainted with the servants and obtained information about Monsieur Hebert's practices.

The parents were in the child's room at a loss for what to do. Marie felt the rags, which ran warm. "These will have to be cooled down as much as possible," Marie said. She sat the child up who appeared lifeless. "Here, sip child." Dorotea appeared to not hear.

"You must drink this, *mon chere*, please for *maman*."

Dorotea drank a tiny sip. "Thatta girl," Madame Hebert said.

"Now, take another sip for *maman.*"

When Monsieur Hebert returned with cooled rags, he sat next to Marie with appreciation in his eyes. "I am so grateful to you for what you're doing for our little girl. Is there anything I can do for you?"

"I just remembered that I had two more appointments today.

I had an appointment with Madame Beauchamp over on First Street. She depends on me. Is there a way to let her know that I cannot go to her home today? I don't want to leave Dorotea."

"Why, I know Madame Beauchamp. I will tell her personally."

"I also have a later appointment with Madame Oubre. She will expect me. I would like her to know I had an emergency. She lives on Second Street with the large hydrangeas in the front."

I will let Madame Oubre know that you are doing a most important job of taking care of my ill daughter."

"Thank you, monsieur."

Marie stayed with Dorotea, feeding her herbal tea and cooling her down with wet cloths the rest of the day and through the night. The next afternoon, Dorotea had improved. Marie stayed with the child two more nights until she was completely well. Monsieur Hebert informed Marie's clients that Marie cured his daughter's fever and soon, the news traveled among the Americans.

Chapter 6

"Did you find out where Monsieur goes on Saturday nights?"

Marie asked Manvil eagerly.

"Yes, Mam'zelle. He goes to the Widow Jardine's home for dinner, and then they go dancing." Manvil spoke happily that he could give Marie the information she wanted.

"Are you sure? Who told you?" Marie's piercing eyes told Manvil that she was desperate to know.

"Moises told me. He drives monsieur to the widow's house and then he picks them up at ten o'clock to go dancing. He never leaves the carriage in front of the widow's house. Then, he picks them up at midnight to take them home."

"Oh, so he doesn't leave his carriage in front of the Widow Jardine's home or in front of the dance hall. Very well, Manvil. You did good. I want you to go to market for me. Buy a boar's head. Tell them not to clean the blood off. Tell them to put it in this black sack. Then, put it in my front yard. It will smell. Go home and rest and in the middle of the night when everyone is asleep, take the black sack with the boar's head and go to the Widow Jardine's home and leave the boar's head on her doorstep. Will you remember to do that, Manvil? Tomorrow is Saturday, the day they go dancing. The boar's head must be on her doorstep tomorrow." She handed Manvil some piasters. "Now, don't whisper a word of this to anyone, not Miss Dehlia or Moises, or they'll come after you." She put her finger to her lips.

Manvil put his finger to his large lips. "I will do as you say, Mam'zel."

Chapter 7

Marie worked very hard, but on Sundays after Mass, she would walk to Congo Square where the slaves were allowed to dance on Sunday afternoons to let off steam. The city saw the Sunday dancing as a "safety valve" to reduce voodoo and other secret gatherings. Often, hundreds of people gathered to watch the frenzied dancers and they became more sensual as the day progressed as the pulse of drums and homemade tambourines grew louder.

Among the vendors who sold refreshments and onlookers sat Jacques Paris enchanted at the sight before him. His heart stuttered when he saw Marie run out and join the women in a circle. Her body moved to the sounds of the Colinda, the favorite dance among the dancers. Her eyes loomed wide as excitement poured through her every shake. Her hips moved far and wide. He couldn't take his eyes off of her. The tom-toms beat and the high-pitched wind instruments whined. She danced to the beat of the rhythm and twirled her body in time with the loudest drum round and round.

His eyes laughed at her as he watched her turn back to the arms of a partner who caught her and twirled her faster and faster, then grabbed her waist and pulled her close to his body. Jacques envied her partner, wishing he could catch her in her twists and turns. He wanted to be with this passionate woman and look into her eyes and touch her fair skin. Yes, he had to figure out a way to be with her and hold her close to his body as the Colinda dancer did.

The high-pitched instruments whined louder and louder, faster and faster, as the dancers danced into a frenzy, moving, swaying, swinging, writhing, thigh beating, chanting, and shaking until they dropped.

Jacques could not contain himself. He had to have this young girl for himself. He wanted to hear her voice.

When the music stopped, Jacques stepped to the edge of the crowd and held his hand out to Marie, as she walked toward him.

She looked up to him inquisitively, breathing heavily from the dancing.

"You danced exquisitely." He smiled into her questioning eyes.

"And you are?" she asked.

"Jacques Paris. I watched your beautiful dancing. May I take you for a drink?"

She did not answer but walked a while out of the crowd.

He followed. "May I, mademoiselle?"

"I am thirsty," she said.

"Then, we'll go right up here to Adan's Tavern."

He escorted her into the tavern where they sat at a table.

"I'm very happy that you've agreed to spend time with me. I work all week up north on the River Road as a carpenter. Saturday and Sunday are my only days to rest. And what do you do?"

"I'm a hairdresser mostly for the Americans. I also nurse the sick when I can."

"That's very charitable of you. This is my first time at Congo Square. And you?"

"I've come here many times," Marie said. "You must not be from here if this is your first time. Where are you from?"

"I was born in Santo Domingo. I've come here to work."

"You must like to work to come all this way," she said.

"Yes, I'm good at what I do."

As Marie talked and relaxed, she agreed to allow Jacques to walk her home, but at the wall in front of her home, she told him, "This is as far as you go."

"When will I see you again?" he asked. "Next Sunday?"

"Perhaps, if I should decide to dance. *Bonne nuit.*"

As Marie was about to open her front door, Manvil stepped out of a bush and approached her. "Manvil, you frightened me. What are you doing here?"

"I come to tell you what happened to Monsieur Hebert."

"Yes, Manvil, tell me."

Moises drove Monsieur to the Widow Jardine's home last night, and she wouldn't let him in the house. He went the time he always go on Saturday and he bang and bang on her door and she don't let him in."

"That's good. That's very good, Manvil." She reached into her pocket. "Here are some coins for some cigarillos. Don't tell Miss Diehlia. Smoke them on my yard, not in her house."

"I see you dancing today. Very pretty." His mouth opened wide, exposing his large, white teeth.

"Never you mind, Manvil." Marie ignored his laugh.

"Pretty dancing, my lady. Hehehehe."

"Go home, Manvil. And remember." She put her finger to her lips.

"Hehehehe. So pretty dancing."

Chapter 8

"Oh, Mawree, you were right that things would change for me," Madame Hebert said, as Marie entered her boudoir.

"I'm happy for you, madame."

"But how did you know?"

"The spirits told me, madame. They are always right. And how is Dorotea? May I see her?"

"She's feeling good and playing with a friend about the house. I'm sure you'll see her before you leave. I'm so grateful to you Marie for getting our daughter well and for, well, you know. Monsieur asked me to give you this for your herbs." She placed five piasters into Marie's palm.

"Oh, no. God lets them grow on my yard to help us and we should help everyone who needs them."

"It's not for the herbs really. It's for all the time you spent with our daughter getting her well when you deserted your hairdressing business. Monsieur and I insist."

"Thank you, madame, for your generosity." Marie put the bills in her pocket.

"Marie, could you sweep my hair up with the curls falling down in the back? Friedrich is taking me dancing tonight. He's been so attentive lately, and staying so close to me, I can hardly believe the change. I got my Friedrich back, Marie."

"Oui, madame." Marie was happy for the glimpse of intimacy she imagined for Madame Hebert and Friedrich.

As she brushed Madame Hebert's long hair, she pomaded it into an upsweep and wrapped it from atop her head around hairgrips (thin wooden sticks) in the back. Marie listened to countless stories of madame's friends. She learned which husband was faithful and which one was not. Of course, Madame Hebert's husband was among the faithful.

As Marie descended the staircase to leave, Dorotea came running to her. "Marie, I fell and hurt my knee in the courtyard." She cried and pointed to her red, scraped knee.

Marie sat on the last step and examined Dorotea's knee.

"I see you have a sore, *mon chere.*"

"Can you fix it? It hurts, Marie."

"Yes, my little one, I can fix it." Marie pulled out a little, cloth bag from her pocket and stuck her finger into it to get a swipe of herbal balm. She gently rubbed it on the child's sore. "See, now it will feel better, and it won't hurt any more. It's all better now, isn't it, *chere?"*

"Yes, Marie, you fixed it." The child looked up to her mother, watching from the landing above. "Mamma, Marie fixed my sore."

"Yes, Marie is a godsend. What would we do without her?"

Chapter 9

Marie saw Jacques every weekend for several months.

He confessed his love for her and asked, "Will you marry me?"

They lay in the shadows of the tall crepe myrtles, their branches filled with deep purple blooms. The damp grass cooled their warm bodies as he held her close, and she felt his hardened manhood. He pressed into her body. She looked up to him and shook her head. "Jacques, I don't think we should..."

Her words slammed him. "Why not? You've told me you love me. We can run away and be married tonight."

"No. We have to do it the right way. I want to talk to my father."

"Are you sure your mother will allow you to marry? You've told me she wants you to have a protector. She probably has one picked out for you, one who will also support her."

"I'll not enter into placage no matter how rich the man is."

He let go of her and rose. "I think your mother has a bigger hold on you than you're aware of. You haven't even invited me to meet her. I never thought that you would not know your own mind, Marie. That was one of the reasons I fell in love with you—because you have a strong will. Will you not marry me because your mother wants something for you that you don't want?"

She stood and held her arms out to him and tenderly embraced him. "Jacques, I will never become a placee. I'm not a slave. I'm free to marry the man I love, and I love you. I want to have babies with you." She kissed him with a passion that soothed him.

"Then, why can't we get married now—tonight?"

"I want to get married in church by my pastor with banns announced and my family present. My father will be in town this week. It will be a perfect time to talk to him about our marriage and ask for his blessing."

"And you must talk to your father for his blessing, a man who has a mistress and a daughter that he sees when he can sneak away from his wife?" Jacques looked away with a grimace.

"Jacques, please don't talk like that about my father. He has been good to my mother and me. I'll tell him I'm in love with the man I want to marry. He always supports me. He will convince my mother. She doesn't feel she can disagree with him. He should be here tomorrow or the day after. Can you come to meet him?"

"You know I have to work." Displeasure marked his face.

She put her hand over his. "Please, be patient with me."

"When would you like to be married?"

"Perhaps, in a month or so."

"That long?" he asked, perturbed.

"I would like to talk to my priest. He will announce the banns in church for three Sundays, and then we may marry."

"If it must be that way, I will wait."

The next day, Marie went to the notary's office. "Bonjour, mademoiselle," the notary welcomed.

"Is my father in town, Monsieur Rousseau?"

"Yes, he is. He asked me to give you this." He handed her an envelope.

"*Bien,* monsieur. And will you please give my father this note?" She handed him a small piece of paper folded.

"I shall, mademoiselle."

"*Au revoir.*" She left the office beaming happily, eyeing the piasters in the envelope.

After Marie left the office, Monsieur Rousseau unfolded Marie's note and read it.

Dear Papa,

I shall make a special dinner for you on Tuesday. Please come. I have something I must talk to you about.

Love,

Marie

As she passed the lively crabs jumping out in buckets and the scaly fish packed in ice crystals sardined between the fruit and vegetable stalls at the French Market, Marie eyed the long whiskers of the catfish and the loins of the goats and purchased the fish and goat for her papa's dinner. She also purchased mirlitons, eggplants, lettuces, cucumbers, tomatoes, and strawberries to top the pound cake. She spent the last of the money he had given her on the best Cuban coffee and fine wine.

She busied herself the next day preparing the dinner for her father.

"Papa, it's so good to see you!" She ran to him and embraced him with all her fervor. He gave her a tight squeeze and smacked her on the cheek. "My p'tite, you look exquisitely happy. I trust you have good news."

He walked over to Marguerite and kissed her on the cheek.

"Marguerite, you are well, I trust."

"Monsieur, I am as well as can be expected."

"Please sit at the table, Papa. I've prepared all of your favorite foods."

"Before we start to eat, Marie, I want to give you this small gift." He handed her a tiny, wrapped box across the table, which she eagerly accepted. "Open it," he said anxiously.

She pulled the wrapping off the box and opened it to find a pair of gold earrings. With eyes wide, she held in tears of joy. "I've never had earrings before. Oh, Papa, thank you." She got up and kissed her father's cheek.

"You spoil the girl." Marguerite said.

"She deserves to be spoiled, and she deserves my love." He noticed thin gold threads in Marie's pierced ear lobes. Marguerite had pierced Marie's lobes but never had enough money to buy her earrings. "I see you have threads in your lobes," he said.

"Oh, yes," Marie said with a laugh.

"We'll have to get rid of the threads and apply your earrings."

Marguerite approached with a paring knife.

"Oh, no! Not that. We need scissors. We could hurt the child with that knife."

Marguerite returned with scissors, and Monsieur Laveau took them from her hand and gently cut the threads from Marie's ear lobes. He, then, placed the golden earrings into Marie's lobes, and Marie glowed as brilliantly as the gold. She moved her head from side to side as her golden hoops dangled and danced. "I will wear these forever."

Marguerite selected morsels of meat and catfish with her shaky, age-spotted hands and placed them on Charles's plate with a sigh and a nod. Monsieur Charles paid no notice as his eyes were on Marie. She looked at the watchful expression of Charles being sweetly entertained by his favorite daughter. She recognized the love he held for Marie in his eyes, eyes she wished he still held for her. He had not come to stay overnight for some time. Marguerite felt a void in her life. She sat quietly pursing her lips and fanning herself with her lace fan as she watched Marie dote over her father, placing vegetables on his plate and pouring his wine.

Charles Laveau turned to his daughter with question in his eyes. What is this important thing you want to talk to me about?"

"I want to be married, Papa. I love him and he loves me."

"I've never even met the man," Marguerite said.

Marie turned to her mother with a frown. "It's because you approve of no man except for a protector who is already married and will only spend time with me when his wife is in a delicate time of month or she has just given birth."

"Is this true, Marguerite? You only want placage for Marie?" Monsieur Laveau asked, surprised at Marie's words of defense.

"I want security for her, to have a home to raise her children in and education for her children," Marguerite shrilled.

"Jacques can provide for me. He is a skilled carpenter.

He works his fingers to the bone and he has saved money. He can build us a home," Marie said.

"Tell me more about this man, Marie," Monsieur Laveau said.

"Jacques Paris is a beautiful quadroon free man of color who works very hard at his craft. He is much in demand as he is a carpenter who works with tongue and groove (no nails) and that is how the rich want their mansions built. He works diligently on the River Road from Monday until the weekend where he comes to the *Vieux Carre* and goes back to work very early on Monday morning. And we can be married in the church, which is what I want."

"Your man sounds intriguing to me." He looked across the table at Marguerite for the first time. "What is your objection, Marguerite?"

"What happens after the houses are built? Where will he work then to support my daughter and her children?"

"I'm sure there will always be a need for houses to be built, Marguerite. And rooms to be added to houses." He smiled toward his daughter.

"And where will they live? Can he provide her with a home like a protector would?" Marguerite thought she had him. Her wrinkled face broke into a cunning smile with a deep nod.

"I own some homes on Bayou Road just outside the *Vieux Carre* and one appears to be empty. I can save it for Marie and Jacques to live in if they so choose." Charles Laveau appeared to be happy to solve the problem of housing for the young couple, but Marguerite was not pleased. She hoped to create a problem to squelch the marriage.

"Thank you, Papa. We will be most pleased to live on Bayou Road."

Marie rose and whispered in her father's ear, spreading her hand in front of his ear so that her mother could not hear. "Papa, please tell *maman* that you approve of the marriage. There is no reason we should not marry."

Charles Laveau beamed proudly. "I give you my blessing, my daughter, for your marriage to Jacques Paris. And I shall give you a lot on Love Street for a wedding present that Jacques may build on in the future."

Marie jumped from her seat, ran to her father, and threw her arms around him. "Thank you, Papa, for my blessing. I love you."

Chapter 10

Her heart sang with joy as she sat in church next to her husband-to-be, listening to her pastor's sermon.

Father Antoine preached. "We are all responsible for a person's sins, and we don't know to what degree we are responsible. The whole community ought to be recognized as partners in moral errors. With better companions, how different one would be." The cathedral, a very plain old pile as described by some with no riches to be seen, was to Father Antoine, a very beautiful place, a peaceful oasis where he could pray and meditate. "And I remind you once again not to judge the placees who are not responsible for their upbringing or circumstances.

I also want to announce the banns of marriage between Santiago Paris, free quadroon, native of Jeremie on the Island of Santo Domingo, resident of this city, natural son of Santiago Paris and Sanite Bleon and Marie Laveau, free woman of color, native and resident of this parish, natural daughter of Carlos

Laveau and Marguerite D'Arcantel," Father Antoine concluded. "In God's name, we pray. Amen."

Marie thrilled at her wedding announcement. She walked out of the cathedral proudly with Jacque's arm entwined around hers.

"I'm so happy, Jacques. It feels official now that I've heard it announced."

"I'm pleased, Marie, to think such a small thing could make you feel so joyous. I only wish I will be able to exude such happiness from you."

Chapter 11

Marie looked beautiful in her lacy, long gown of apricot color with hues of orange peeping through the lace at intervals, her satin slippers matching. She walked proudly next to her father, Charles Laveau, as her dream to marry came true. She knew very few young women of color who realized their dream of marrying as there were more free women of color than free men of color. And many had placage chosen for them. Even her mother never had the privilege of marrying in the church.

The sanctuary smelled like a flower garden. Marie's homemade incense balm was dabbed on the back of every female wrist in the cathedral.

Jacques stood patiently, waiting for Marie at the altar in French coat and cravat. He looked to Marie with longing in his dark, shiny eyes. She went to stand next to him, showing love in her expression. They knelt on cushioned kneelers as Father Antoine started the celebration of Nuptial Mass after which he had Marie and Jacques recite their vows.

Marie's mother, half-sisters, nieces, and cousins in rainbow colored tignons dotted the cathedral, as they looked on with tears in their eyes. Marie's tignon stood out among theirs in cranberry red colors interspersed with orange, apricot, cherry red, and green wrapped around her head in seven points.

Father Antoine pronounced Marie and Jacques "Man and Wife." Jacques reached down and gently kissed his newly wedded wife.

Marie walked out of the cathedral in ecstasy, her arm around her husband. Her half-sister gave a silent clap.

The family filled the one and a half story weather-beaten tile-roofed cottage, bringing loads of food and wine. Her relatives and neighbors filled her long wooden table with crawfish, rice, etoufees of every description, vegetables, and berries. They ate and sang in every room in the house. The back doors of the cottage were thrown open to the patio in the autumn breeze, and they moved to the back yard to play their drums and violins, dancing and singing into the evening.

Jacques was enthralled with the idea of being married to Marie rather than the celebration. He tired in the evening and asked Marie if they could leave the fete for their new, bequeathed home on Bayou Road.

"Please, Marie, we only have two nights together, and then I'll have to leave you for work very early on Monday morning."

"I understand, Jacques, but I hope that *mere* will."

Marie went to her boudoir to change into a cotton shift and threw some belongings into a canvas bag. She went to her mother. *"Mere,* we will be leaving now."

Marguerite threw a look of disappointment. "I thought you would be in our home tonight, at least for a few days. Our family will return tomorrow to finish up all the food. Will you be back?"

"I don't know. We only have tonight and tomorrow and then Jacques has to leave for work."

"But I thought you would furnish your home before you move. Do you have furniture?"

"Mere, we don't need furniture. We're in love." Marie kissed her mother's forehead in farewell.

He led her into their cottage by candlelight and held her hand until they entered the boudoir. Placing the lit candle into a candlestick on a small table in the corner, he pointed to blankets on the floor in the middle of the room. "I haven't been able to buy a bed yet, *chere,* but I will next week when I return from work. I hope you won't mind sleeping on the floor until next week."

"I don't mind, Jacques. I know you will keep me comfortable, sleeping close to me."

"That I will, *mon chere.* Oh, I'm so happy." He lifted her from the floor and swung her around. "We have our whole life to furnish this place and to fill it with family. But tonight, it's just the two of us here together. I want to make love to you, Marie." He guided her to the blanket on the floor. Leaning over her, he removed her drawers and kissed her, running his hands up and down her body.

A quick succession of drum beats slower than a roll sounded outside. His love words stilled the paradiddles wafting in the cool wind and the batten shutters banging against the cottage.

She also did not hear the violins stringing outside. She only heard Jacques' love words, the words she waited for from him.

He rose and walked to a dark corner and dropped his clothes. His passion begged to come out of his body as he came toward her in the darkened room. He breathed in the grassy scent of her hair and felt a rush of tenderness for her and wanted her more than he ever felt he could want a woman.

Kissing her and feeling her body, he wished that he could stop time. His passion spiraled until he was in another world so pure, overwhelmingly happy as he had never been. The room seemed to lift as he piqued into total ecstasy.

He started to enter her and looked down at this sensuous woman he had admired for so long. He could hardly believe this was real. She let him love her as he had always wanted to love her, and she looked happy.

He thought he'd never be able to stop thrusting and when he did, he looked down on her still in her passion. He tried to stop his heart from pounding and waited for her. She looked so beautiful, and finally she stopped her heavy breathing and appeared satisfied just to look up to him and kiss him.

"I love you, *mon cherie*. You are my life," he moaned, breathing heavily.

"*Cherie, Je t'adore,*" she whispered.

After two days of lovemaking, he told her he had to leave her to go up north to build a great plantation home. "I will not be able to come home to you every night, although I would love to be with you and make love to you. It is such a long distance, Cherie. But I will come home next Saturday, and I will buy a bed for us and you will be more comfortable sleeping in it. We will go to mass together on Sunday. Afterwards, perhaps we will go dancing. I look forward to holding you in my arms and looking into your beautiful eyes and dancing with you."

Jacques rose before daybreak and rumbled in a one horse wooden wagon on muddy roads past cypress swamps and sugar cane fields along Louisiana's Great River Road to work on spacious mansions of the rich planters who owned plantations along the winding river and townhouses in the city.

Chapter 12

Marie's neighbor on Bayou Road happened to be Christophe de Glapion, a former soldier in the army. Having noticed him in his full dress uniform, she had admired him walking tall and proud.

He greeted her on the banquette one morning, as she left for work. "*Bonjour,* madame," he greeted with a full smile. He tipped his hat, delighted that she had nodded toward him.

"*Bonjour,*" Marie sang and went on her way in her blue gingham skirt flowing around her ankles, her gold earrings dangling.

He looked after her for a long time, as she walked toward Canal Street in her assured manner. She had a way of walking, straight and tall, and people noticed her.

Monsieur Glapion could not get Marie out of his mind. Her attractive looks and unavailability intrigued him. He knew she was married and also realized she was lonely. Night after night, he would see her come home alone to an empty house. Her husband appeared to be absent. He wondered why this was.

He decided to pay a call on Marie one night. After knocking on her door, she appeared in the doorway. "I noticed your lamp on. I know it's of a late hour but uh…"

"Yes. I'm still up and about," she said with a smile.

"I live…" He motioned to his home.

"Next door. Yes, I know."

"Is there anything? I mean…" He cleared his throat.

"I just wanted to let you know, as a neighbor, madame, if I can be of service to you in any way, I am here to help. Do you need anything?"

"My needs are quite limited. I'm quite independent, you know. Would you like to come in for a moment, monsieur?"

Her parlor seemed silent and lifeless until he looked at Marie, looking back at him with large, penetrating eyes that told him she was happy for the company.

His nostrils filled with the smell of her homemade incense, as she welcomed him with a smile. He noticed the smoke trail up from a small dish on a table, as he removed his hat.

"I see you go to work every day and come home at a late hour."

"Yes, my hours are long."

"As a neighbor, I want you to know that I'm here to assist you in any way. My intentions are quite honorable, madame."

"I've no doubt, monsieur."

He looked back at her and wondered if she felt the same attractiveness for him as he felt for her.

Her eyes would not stay on him.

"Your resourcefulness and diligence is quite obvious, madame. And may I be so bold as to say you are also quite beautiful?"

His words almost took her breath away. She took notice of him as an attractive man for some time, and these were words she had not heard in her recent memory. Her eyes spoke to him of appreciation.

He understood the look. "Do I see tears in your eyes, madame? Are you sad tonight?"

"Oh, no," she denied, dismissing her feelings.

"And what do you hear of your husband?"

"He works on the River Road, you know. He is a carpenter much in demand, as he works with tongue and groove. He's hired to build the bones of a plantation house. Coming back and forth is too long a distance."

"I understand. I should leave you now to rest." He rose to leave and walked toward her. She put her hand out to him. He took it and pressed his lips fervently on the top of it. She stepped back quickly, not expecting such a kiss with a faint feeling of embarrassment. He reached for her, as he thought she might be swooning and held her in his arms. She looked up to him and stared into his eyes. They stood quietly, as he held her. *How wonderful to feel her in my arms. This must be how heaven feels.*

As he held her in his arms, she felt the warmth she had longed for. *Oh, how I loved hearing those words from a man. You are so wonderful to say them to me. I needed to hear what you said on this lonely night.*

The parlor door was thrust open with a bang. Jacques stood with horror in his eyes, as he spied Marie in the arms of another man.

Marie and Christophe broke their embrace and faced Jacques. "Good evening, husband," Marie greeted.

Christophe, wanting to be cordial, walked toward him and put out his hand.

Jacques's eyes flashed fire and darted toward him and held an angry stare at Marie. "And who are you?" he asked Christophe with incriminating eyes. His face flushed with fury, and his voice rasped. "What are you doing with my wife?"

"I am your neighbor, monsieur. I was just asking madame if I might be of service to her."

"I see that you offered more than she needs. I must ask you to leave, monsieur."

Marie walked toward her husband for an embrace. "He meant well, Jacques. He only wanted to help me."

Jacques ignored her advances with sharp eyes on Christophe. "And you defend this man and take sides against me?"

"No, Jacques. I am not taking sides."

She heard a strange tone in his voice that she had not heard before, not the warm voice she was used to.

"I'm sorry I gave such a bad impression. I will leave you to your wife. *Bonne nuit.*"

Jacques stared at Christophe with piercing eyes that shouted, as Christophe left the parlor.

"Bonne nuit," Marie said.

Jacques drew his lower teeth out and blew breath from his mouth. She heard the air blow in and out like a dragon blowing fire. For the first time in their marriage, she felt fear, as he came face to face with her, his shoulders squared.

"I left my work to come home to be with you and find you in the arms of another man. Is this how you spend your time when I'm away working?" He stared at her with shining eyes.

"No! I work, too, and bring money home every day."

"You have humiliated me, Marie. Do the neighbors see him coming in and out of our home?"

Her troubled eyes saw the color drained from his face.

"Answer me," he roared.

She shook her head in denial. "No! This is the first time he has paid a call. He was just trying to be nice to me. It's because I'm always alone. He wanted to see if I was in need of anything."

His face puffed up with rage. "In need of anything?" "Don't I provide for your needs, working my fingers to the bone?"

"Of course, you do, Jacques. It's not about money."

"Then what is it about, Marie? The comfort of his arms?"

"No! He was just being kind to me." She backed away from him, feeling the heat of his anger.

"I can't trust you to be faithful to me when I'm gone. I never thought you, Marie, of all people," he droned.

His words sliced through her. "I have never been unfaithful to you, Jacques. I love you!" she shouted.

"Yes, you love me," he said with deep contempt.

His spiteful words brought tears to her eyes. "I do! I love you with all my heart."

They dueled with his jealous questions and her defensive answers until she fell to the floor in tears, begging him to stop. "Why don't you believe me? I never betrayed you," she screamed. Her sobs stopped his accusations, as he stared down at her.

His piercing stare shone at her watery eyes in the glow of the candle's red flame.

She tried to gentle him from his fury, reaching for his hand to squelch the fiery rage within him.

"Humph! Maybe we should move so that your neighbor won't be near you to come and assist you every time you need comforting," he raved. His smirk slid from his face.

"Anything you want, Jacques. Anything."

Silent fury flared inside of him as he slammed the door and stormed from the cottage. Marie sat frozen, drained from the fiery scene of accusations. Her light, tan face contorted with worry, as she rocked herself from side to side.

Sadness took over her. *Mon Dieu, what just happened? In a matter of minutes, he came to be with me and now he is gone. Will he come back?*

Chapter 13

After Jacques left, Marie spent the next winter wondering if her husband would return. Loneliness took over her. Christophe also did not visit her, and she began to wish he would come to her home, first for companionship and then, she longed for some affection. She wondered at these feelings and tried to dismiss them.

She thought of Christophe's sea-blue eyes and wavy brown hair against his white skin, so unusual to her, and his army uniform that he occasionally wore for formal occasions. Marie had never seen such a striking figure of a man.

She saw him through her rain-washed window, walking by and turning his head to get a glimpse of her. He walked by her window often. She knew he wanted to see her.

In her loneliness, she craved her father's attention and decided to go to the notary to inquire when her father would be in town.

"Bonjour, monsieur. Have you heard from my papa?"

Monsieur Roussel looked down at some papers on his desk, giving him time to decide how to break the bad news to Marie. "Please, Marie, sit here."

Nearing his desk, she felt sadness fall upon the room. She sat and waited.

He looked at her and spoke quietly. "Marie, your papa has passed away. I am so sorry, you dear child. I know how much you loved him. Oh, and I know he loved you, too. I remember how happy he was when he came to see you and your mother. He spoke of you endlessly. The man loved you. I know." He nodded.

Marie looked away and would not let the tears flood that she held back. "Did he leave a note?"

"No, I'm sorry, dear child, he did not. He would have if he had the chance, but he went so fast."

She rose unsteadily and braced herself against the armchair. "You have served my mother and father and me ever since I was a mere child. Thank you ever so much, monsieur."

Marie walked toward the river through the Vieux Carre under curly wrought iron balconies, some with wet laundry basking in the tropical New Orleans heat. Latin faces looked down at her above cafes, patisseries, and taverns. She hid her broken heart as she walked in the veil of heat and humidity, looking cool and undisturbed despite the stares of men, past the shop of the mender of broken combs. She wondered if she should tell her mother the terrible news since her mother had taken to her bed as of late with chest pains. She decided to go to her mother but not sure if she should tell her that the love of her life will not visit her again, those visits that kept her mother alive.

Not feeling she wanted to face her mother just yet, she decided to go home and rest awhile and let her feelings out in the privacy of her boudoir. As she rested in her bed and wept, she heard a knock on her door. Upon answering, an unfamiliar woman appeared with her plump daughter. Before Marie could inquire, the woman set her foot across the threshold and entered, her daughter following without invitation.

"I've come to take some of our belongings—the ones I can carry with me today," she said.

"And you are?" Marie inquired.

"I am Madame Charles Laveau. And this is my daughter, Marie Dolores," she said with a snide smile.

Marie nodded to her half-sister. They passed her without the least recognition.

Madame Charles Laveau spied a painting on the wall with haughty effrontery. "No doubt that came from Charles who you claim to be your father." She reached for the frame, but it was quite above her reach.

Marie simply said, "They were not given to me by my father. The Chief of Police gave two of these paintings to us as a wedding gift."

Madame Charles Laveau harrumphed under her breath and gave Marie a sour look. She spied the antique tables and kerosene lamps.

"The Chief of Police will vouch for me if you want."

"That won't be necessary," Madame Laveau let out in a loud voice.

Noticing Madame Laveau's eyes fastened on a beautiful crystal candlestick, Marie replied, "That was a gift from Madame Oebre. It's very rare with its slight tinge of pink in the globe. I work across Canal Street as a hairdresser, you know, and they pay me very well. The American ladies were most generous when I married."

Marie allowed Madame Laveau and her daughter to lead her into her boudoir as if it belonged to them. She saw Madame Laveau's lustful stare at her bed, as she pointed archly to it.

"And where did that come from, may I inquire? Also from the Chief of Police?"

"My husband purchased it. We have the receipt."

"And where is he?" Madame Laveau turned to Marie with a lifted eyebrow.

"He builds plantation homes on the River Road."

As Madame Laveau passed Marie's looking glass, she saw her reflection and turned her head this way and that way in order to admire herself, brushing back her swept up hair. Her daughter passed the looking glass and did likewise.

Leaving the boudoir, Madame Laveau could not hide the disappointment in her face. She wanted to pull Marie's looking glass off the wall but thought of The Chief of Police and stopped. "You will have to be out of the house by tomorrow. I have another tenant who will move in the day after."

"My father is barely cold, and I have not gotten used to the idea that he is gone. How can you have another tenant ready so soon?"

"Don't you know these cottages are in demand? I can't worry that you've no place to go. We need the house!"

"Certainly, you can give me time to pack," Marie said with a sinking heart.

"Pack? You'll be evicted! Your things will be out in the road. The things you say are gifts." She grinned with scorn, showing her large teeth.

"Even evicted parties are given notice. Surely, my father wouldn't have wanted this. He wanted me to be happy."

"I don't know what your father wanted for you. I only know you have to be out of here by tomorrow or your things will be thrown out in the road and confiscated."

Marie led the women out of her cottage with a satisfying feeling that she had kept her composure.

Marie's neighbor, Colonel Christophe Glapion's mother, saw Madame Charles Laveau coming from Marie's cottage through her window and seized the opportunity for some gossip. "Madame, may I address you?" She took on an air of humility for the first time in her life. "I am Madame Glapion, a neighbor, and I see her goings on." She pointed to Marie's cottage.

"I am Madame Marie Francoise Fanchon Dupart Laveau, the owner of the house she lives in, and this is my daughter, Mademoiselle Marie Dolores."

"I am so pleased to make your acquaintances," Madame Glapion said, smiling, and noticing that Madame Laveau put on airs and was a *griffe* (darker skinned.) "I must tell you that the hairdresser is a married woman whose husband is rarely here. Where he goes, God only knows." Her eyes lifted up to the heavens. "My son, Christophe, and the hairdresser here have taken on together." She pointed her head toward Marie's cottage.

Madame Laveau gave a horrifying look. Her daughter gasped and put her chubby hands to her mouth. "Tsk, tsk," came from their lips.

"Yes, yes, I know it's hard to believe, but I've seen it with my very own eyes. It's a shame a mother has to witness such goings on."

Madame Laveau threw a look of disgust. "How dreadful. Her father would turn over in his grave if he only knew! Maybe even disown her."

"Yes, I'm quite sure," Madame Glapion agreed. "I just thought I'd warn you."

"Does your son know she's married?"

"Why, I uh... He hasn't really discussed her with me. I was wondering, madame, if you and your daughter would like to have coffee with me some time? I am a widow, and I'd love to have you and your daughter over for some serious conversation."

"How gracious of you. I am also recently widowed and only here at my townhouse occasionally, but I'd love to see you when I'm in town to talk with you."

"Can you come day after tomorrow? I'm sure I'll have the latest news to discuss with you."

"Yes, madame. Thank you for the invitation. The eviction should be over by then."

"Eviction?! Why, I never thought... Oh, my goodness, that is news! Then, I will expect you and your daughter on Thursday afternoon at four. *Au revoir.*"

Marie had no time to weep although her heart was breaking. She hurried to the police station to talk to her friend, Monsieur Hebert."

"I must speak to the Chief of Police," she said.

"And who may I ask wishes to speak to him," the clerk asked.

"Madame Marie Laveau Paris. He knows me. I work for his wife."

"Ah, yes, he's mentioned you. I'll see if he's available."

The clerk returned and directed Marie to monsieur's office.

The Chief of Police looked up from his desk and gave Marie a warm smile. "Marie, please sit. What can I do for you?"

"Monsieur, I have a big problem. I just received news today from the notary that my dear father has passed away." Marie spoke in a cracked voice and let out a sob.

"I'm very sorry to hear that, Marie."

"His wife just came to my cottage and tried to take my belongings from my home. Even the paintings you generously gave us for a wedding present."

Monsieur Hebert slapped his hand on his desk and let out a roar. "Never!"

"And she says I have to be out of the cottage by tomorrow or I will be evicted and my belongings will be thrown out in the road and will be confiscated. I said I needed time to pack my things, and she scorned me."

"That will never happen, Marie. How far are you behind with the rent?"

"There never was rent. My father owned the cottage and he gifted me the place to live in as part of my dowry plus a lot on Love Street. He wanted us to live on Bayou Road until my husband could build a home on Love Street. This is not what my father wanted. Believe me."

"I believe you, Marie." He stood and paced, keeping silent for a moment as he thought of his next move. "There will be no eviction. There was never a notice to pay rent. I will have two policemen guard your home. If anyone tries to break in and move possessions out of your home, they will be arrested."

"Can you do that for me, monsieur?"

"That I can. I will have two of my men drive you home and guard the place. How many days do you need to pack?"

"I expect it would be nice to have two or three days to pack my things."

"Good. On Saturday morning, I'll send a wagon to move you. Do you have a place? If not, find one. If you can't find a place, let one of my men know and he'll get a message to me, and I'll see what I can do to find something."

"I'll move to my family home in the *Vieux Carre.*"

"Good, Marie. Then, we're all set."

A wagon pulled up to Marie' cottage, and two black servants of Madame Laveau's ran up to Marie's door with key in hand. As one man turned the key to enter with one foot on the threshold, a policeman grabbed him from behind and cuffed him. He also cuffed his partner at his side.

"You are arrested for breaking and entering in an attempt to rob," the policeman said.

"I ain't no robber. I have a key to this place. See?" He held up the key as if the key would absolve him.

"It doesn't matter if you have a key. This is a private home, and it's not yours. Sydney, take them in and book them. I'll watch the house."

As Sydney pulled the two servants onto the police wagon, they yelled back, "Our boss owns this house. Madame Laveau. She told us to come and put her things out on the road. Ask her. Boy, are you ever in trouble with her."

Evening was approaching, and Madame Laveau began to wonder why her servants didn't report back to her that they had vacated Marie's cottage. She decided to go to the cottage.

When she arrived, she saw her horse and wagon in front but no sign of her servants or Marie's belongings. She did the same as her servant and turned the lock with her key and entered Marie's home. The policeman happened to be inside.

"Madame, you are under arrest for breaking and entering."

"How dare you! I am the owner of this house, monsieur."

"You may own this house, but this happens to be the private home of a tenant. You can't break into a tenant's home, and you can't attempt to take her belongings, which I'm told you did attempt to do. Please, step outside, madame."

He walked her outside. "You can make this easy for yourself and go peacefully with me or you can attempt to run away in which case I will catch you and handcuff you and the neighbors will get an eyeful of you being arrested."

"I'll go with you, but we'll see about that. It's all a mistake."

At the police station, Madame Laveau was booked for illegal breaking and entering. She was led to a jail cell. "You can't be serious! I wish to speak to your superior at once."

"I'll tell him you're here, madame."

The Chief of Police, Monsieur Hebert, came to Madame Laveau's cell. "You asked to speak to me?"

"Why, yes. Why is it that you locked me up like a criminal when I attempted to enter my own house?"

"It's because your intentions were not to help your tenant, who had just heard that very day that she lost her father, but to steal her possessions. I happen to know that Marie Laveau Paris is a very hardworking, young woman and works for everything that she has, as well as her husband. She has worked tirelessly to nurse people with yellow fever and has nursed many children to health, as well as my own daughter. To think that you would take from her is a despicable act."

Madame Laveau squeezed her hands and moved her head from side to side. "Well, I never really knew Marie. My late husband had a liaison with her mother, and I didn't know them."

"It was more than a liaison, madame. He had a child with her and supported her mother and Marie for her entire life. From what Marie has told me, he truly loved Marie and her mother."

Madame Laveau squirmed in her seat, showing displeasure in her flushed cheeks. "Well, I didn't take anything."

"Only because the police stopped your servants and you. You instructed your servants to steal from her and destroy her property."

"When can I get out of this horrible place?"

"When someone bails you out.

"How will my daughter know I am here? Can you get a message to her?"

"Yes. I'll have a notice posted on several lampposts in the Vieux Carre saying that Madame

Marie Francoise Fanchon Dupart Laveau was arrested for breaking and entering and is in the county jail. The news will travel fast, and I'm sure your daughter will find out where you are."

Madame Laveau screamed in horror. "You can not do this. You can not!" Her screams echoed through the jailhouse.

Marie Dolores followed the jailer to her mother's jail cell to release her. As she witnessed her mother through iron bars, she let out gasps of horror and screamed, "Mama!"

"Oh, my dear daughter. I waited an eternity for you to find me. How horrible it is to be in this hell hole."

"I am told I must pay your bail before they will release you. I will pay it and come back for you, Mama. Oh, how dreadful it is to see you in that cell," she cried out.

The daughter returned with the jailer. "Come, Mama, let us get you home. The carriage is waiting for us." Marie Dolores guided her mother from the cell down a dank gangway as they found their way out into the brightness of a sunny day.

As they reached their way to the road, a coachman aided Madame Charles Laveau into the carriage. "Take us to 25 Bayou Road!" she demanded. "It's between Rampart and St. Claude."

"Mama, why are we going there? Don't you want to go home and rest after your ordeal?" Marie Dolores looked puzzled.

"Rest? Ah, no, my child, I can't wait to talk to Madame Glapion. We have much to discuss."

As Madame Glapion opened her front door, Madame Charles Laveau appeared on her doorstep. "I'm truly sorry to intrude at this late hour, madame, but I must speak to you regarding your neighbor."

"Please, do come in, madame."

As Madame Laveau and her daughter entered Madame Glapion's sitting room, Madame Glapion lit the candles.

"I must tell you that the rumors regarding your neighbor and her voodoo most certainly must be true. Otherwise, why would they have arrested me instead of her?"

"Arrested? No!" Madame Glapion's eyes lit up in anticipation of more gossip.

"I came this afternoon to check on my home next door. I am the owner, you know." A mocking smile left her lips. "Well, there's no other explanation. It's voodoo, I tell you. She puts spells on people. I just had to warn you."

Madame Glapion looked toward Marie's cottage with a worried look as if she could see danger. "I'm most certainly happy for the information. I must warn my son."

Madame Charles Laveau's gossip pitchforked into a coil of scandal and spread throughout the community.

Marie's defiant spirit led her to ignore the unflattering rumors that Madame Laveau and Madame Glapion passed around the neighborhood.

Christophe Glapion admired this strength in Marie in that she went about her business as usual. She went to work every day and greeted Madame Glapion when she met her in the street as if the woman had not tried to blacken her name. Marie had her own way of dealing with people. And Christophe began to feel tender love for Marie when his mother would laugh and tell him that Marie greeted her as if she were a friend.

Chapter 14

As Marie walked through the cottage, she found her mother in bed. Marguerite's sunken eyes and ghostly face alarmed Marie. "Mama, are you not feeling well?"

"No, Daughter. I have the pains in my chest again. Can you give me something for that?"

"Show me, Mama. Where does it hurt?"

Marguerite laid her palm on her chest.

"I think that Juanita, the Indian woman, has exactly what I need. I'll go and ask her, Mama. You just rest."

Marie went out to her yard to find an Indian woman resting on the ground with her papoose in a basket. "Juanita, I need herbs for my mama. Her heart is bothering her. Chest pains."

"I hope this helps your mother's heart," she said with sadness." The Indian woman handed the herbs in a little black sack to Marie with uncertainty in her expression, not the happy smile she usually had when she'd say, "Here madame, this should most certainly cure your person." Juanita had witnessed Marguerite grimacing in pain and clutching her chest for some time.

"Thank you, Juanita. You are most kind."

Marie brewed the herbs and spoon-fed the tea to her mother with the gnawing feeling that the herbs would not heal her mother's ailing heart. She sat with her mother as she lay dying and knew she could not keep death away and accepted that her mother's time had come. Still grieving for her father, she did not have the heart to tell her mother that her father had passed. She had asked Manvil to get Father Antoine to administer the last rites.

As Marie sat with her dying mother in the summer heat under low adobe walls with steam dripping down, Marguerite had told her stories she had not heard before, stories of healing when Marguerite was a fever nurse, a hoodoo doctor, and a voodoo practitioner. As a young girl, Marie had aided her mother in nursing the wounded in the War of 1812. She learned how to heal the infected wounds and bandage the soldiers.

They looked forward to the evening when they welcomed a light breeze rambling through the cottage.

"I have only one regret," Marguerite said. "I shouldn't have let you see how we had to cut the arms and legs off of soldiers when you were so very young. It was a horrible sight. Nothing for a child to see." Tears filled Marguerite's eyes.

"Pay no mind to that, Mama. It made me strong. But I do still dream about it sometimes."

"I've no doubt, it has made you strong. You're the strongest woman I know. I remember how you hated to clean the bed pans and the vomit," Marguerite said to her daughter with her last smile. "But that taught you humility and how to care for those who needed you. And now you're taking care of me."

"Yes, Mama. Now, I'll take care of you. Just rest."

"I have one more thing to tell you, Marie."

"Yes, Mama?"

"I don't know if you remember. You were so very young. You had yellow fever as a child. We almost lost you. I hate to think of it. Your father and I cried at your bedside to think that you might die. He helped to get ice every day to cool you down and went to the pharmacy on Chartres Street to purchase anything the pharmacist would recommend besides the herbs I was giving you. Poor man. I never saw him so distraught. He prayed as I never saw him pray before. And then you know what happened?"

"What, Mama?"

"God gave us a gift. He made you well and gave you something very special."

Marie looked down at her mother with questioning eyes.

"God gave you the gift of immunity." Marguerite lifted her dying head off of her pillow and looked straight into Marie's eyes. "And you must not take that gift for granted. Very few people get that gift from God. You must help people with the fever because you will not catch that horrible disease."

"I will, Mama. I promise."

"And one more thing. I know you have been a good sister to your half-sister and half-brother. They were born long before you were from a different father, but they are the closest kin you have. Be good to them and take care of them when they are sick. Also their children. I'm sure they'll be in need of you some time in the future."

"I will, Mama. Don't you worry about that."

"I am certain that you will take care of your family. And when your loving father should ever need you, offer him your home and nurse him. I know he would love to spend his last days with you. It would mean so much to him. You know that you were his favorite daughter."

Marie stifled a sob. *Oh, how I wish I could have taken care of him.* "Just rest, Mama. You don't need to worry about a thing."

"I know, my child. Don't ever forget the gift that God gave you."

Death came stealing her mother away one warm June morning. Marie had woken in a chair next to her mother's bed with the sun shining in her face. She got up and felt her mother's stone-cold hand. Her body lay lifeless and cold. Marie closed her mother's eyes and knelt to pray for her mother's soul and ran for Father Antoine to prepare for the funeral. Father Antoine comforted Marie as the best friend that he was.

Chapter 15

After her mother's death, Marie lived a lonely life in her mother's weather-beaten cottage alone. She'd open the heavy batten-window shutters in the morning and stare out, mourning for her mother and aching for her husband. Wanting the comfort of her father, she would start to write a note to him inviting him to come and visit her, and then she'd remember that he was gone also. She cried for her father's passing and would give anything she had to see him just one more time. She acquired more patrons to make the lonely hours shorter, keeping very busy.

As Marie left for work towards Canal Street, men turned to admire her rhythmic gate with her blue denim skirt twirling around her ankles. Some stopped to look at her striking features with admiration, but Marie did not notice or nod this morning. She thought of Madame DuPont's problems that always seemed to become Marie's problems. Marie coiffured madame's hair and solved her medical problems, but it was her personal problems that Marie spent more time solving.

Marie disdained the luxurious idleness of the Americans who lived on the other side of Canal Street, also their ostentatious homes and showy gardens in the front of their houses. Marie considered this showing off.

She witnessed the lap of luxury that Madame DuPont lived in and did not envy her but reviled her frivolous life-style. She secretly groaned when she entered Madame DuPont's boudoir. The absence of an altar in madame's boudoir always set her back. Instead, madame had a mirrored dressing table with copious fluted bottles of colognes and perfumes. The scents did not always please Marie.

"Marie, I could scarcely wait for you to come today. Please, sit here." She pointed to a heavily upholstered chair in purple velvet.

Before Marie could set herself down, Madame DuPont went on to address her problem. "Marie, I am wondering where all of our money is going. Monsieur tells me his business is failing. At first, I sympathized with him and asked my father to subsidize our income, but then I looked at the business's books one afternoon when he was away. God only knows where he goes in the afternoons. Do you think he has another woman?"

"I don't know, madame."

"Well, the business is doing fine and no matter how much my father gives him, he does not put it into the business. He spends it and tells me we're out of money. What do you think, Marie? I hear among my circles that you're very good at figuring these things out."

"I'll have to pray about this and ask the spirits where the money goes."

"Do you think you can help me?"

"Yes, I know I can."

"Oh, Marie, I value our friendship so much. You'll never know. Now, I must tell you how I want my hair fixed for a very special event I'm attending."

Marie found Manvil on her yard, smoking cigarillos.

"Manvil, I need you to help me."

"Yes, madame. Anything." Manvil was pleased that Marie would give him money for cigarillos every time he helped her, and he was able to leisurely smoke them on her yard.

"I need you to follow an American man, Monsieur DuPont, and tell me where he goes."

"Yes, madame."

"We will take a carriage to his home across Canal Street. I will leave you off there, and you follow him when he goes out for his nightly jaunt. Then, tomorrow, follow him when he goes out in the afternoon."

"I can do that, madame."

"Good, Manvil. Come back and tell me where he goes in the afternoon and at night."

Manvil crept like a thief in the night, hiding behind bushes and pillars as he followed Monsieur DuPont in the dark to the cockfights on the edge of town. Manvil became so interested in the cockfights, he almost forgot to keep his eye on Monsieur DuPont who was gambling excitingly amid lit candles. Money flew back and forth on the ground between each contest of the gamecocks fitted with metal spurs. Manvil found it all very exciting. He hated to leave when he had to follow Monsieur DuPont home.

In the morning, Manvil hid in a comfortable hiding place under a porch next to monsieur's grand home and waited until the rich American left his home. He followed the man uptown to the lottery ticket office. Manvil wasn't sure what this building was, but he remembered what it looked like and later took Marie to see it.

"See, that's where monsieur went in, right there."

"I see that that's the lottery ticket office. You've done very well, Manvil. It all makes sense."

Manvil shrugged his shoulders, not understanding what the building represented.

"Here Manvil." She put piasters onto Manvil's welcoming palms. "You can buy cigarillos but don't tell Diehlia."

"Have the spirits guided you, Marie?" Madame DuPont asked.

"Yes, madame."

"Well, where does my husband go in the afternoons?"

"Your husband has been gambling at the lottery ticket office."

"Oh, my God in heaven. Has he been squandering the family's money on gambling?"

"Yes, madame."

"Well, at least it's not on a woman, is it not?"

"Yes, madame, it is not on a woman."

"Oh, Marie, you don't know how relieved I am. I owe you so much. You're a godsend. But I don't know where that lottery ticket office is. Do you?"

"Yes, madame."

"Can you take me there?"

"Yes, madame. It is not far. It is uptown."

Madame DuPont clapped her hands, and a maid appeared. "Beulah, tell my driver to meet me out front. We are going uptown."

The coachman stopped in front of the lottery ticket office when Marie pointed it out to him. "This is it, madame."

"Marie, will you go in with me? I've never been in a place like this."

"Of course, madame. You just go in and tell them you are Madame DuPont and you want to check the DuPont receipts. That way you can verify your husband's gambling."

Marie guided madame DuPont into the building and directed her to the proper person. "Remember what I told you, madame. They will know your name."

As Marie stepped off the stoop outside the lottery ticket office, she came face to face with Monsieur DuPont. He looked as surprised as Marie. "Marie! What are you in God's name doing here?"

"I came with madame. She is inside."

"But how did she know?"

"The spirits."

He was taken aback with widening eyes as if something had struck him. "Then…What they say about you is true. I would never have believed it but…she knows?"

"Yes, monsieur. She knows you gamble."

"Did you also tell her about the cockfights?"

"No, monsieur, but if she asks…"

"Please, don't tell her. Please. You'll break up our marriage if you do." He grasped her hand and placed piasters into it.

"I would never break up your marriage, monsieur. That is not my intent."

"Thank you, Marie."

"Bonjour." She watched him enter the building a shaken man.

Chapter 16

Marie worked tirelessly but on Sunday, she would take a respite. After mass, she walked to Congo Square to watch the slaves dance the Bamboula in their striking moves amid the pulse of drums. It helped Marie to dissuade mourning her mother and father and missing the arms of her husband.

In the past, she would have run out to dance with the men and women in a frenzied dance that would make her feel sensual. Her uninhibited moves would make her happy, exuding excitement to those all around her. She would encourage many to join her as slaves and free people of color were allowed to dance on these Sunday afternoons. But at sunset, the slaves had to depart for home.

Now, she sat alone merely watching. A young black boy came to her and asked, "Madam, would you like a lemonade, orangeade, or a barley-water?"

"No, thank you." She smiled at the boy and noticed his tattered clothes.

"Perhaps, a glass of wine? I can get it for you."

Marie could not ignore his pleading eyes. "No, thank you, but here." She handed him a handful of Spanish piasters left over from her marketing.

"He bowed in thanksgiving. "Thank you. God bless you."

She spotted his uniform and his special gait with his shoulders pushed back and his back straight. *It's him.*

No one else walks like that. She felt exhilarated and excited. She watched Christophe Glapion walking and spying the crowd as if he were looking for someone. She wondered if he was looking for a woman.

He turned and spotted her sitting in the crowd and brimmed his hat toward her and gave a nod.

Marie's heart stopped, and she turned to look the other way, pretending she didn't see him, but she knew he saw her staring at him.

She tired of sitting alone and decided to leave. As she made her way home, she heard his words.

He spotted her leaving and decided to catch up with her. "Good evening, madame."

As she turned, his eyes were there to meet her, and he greeted her warmly with a look of admiration "You look lovely. Take my arm, madame. There are many potholes here. I wouldn't want you to fall."

She smiled and took his arm and couldn't help thinking that Jacques had never been so concerned with her safety, never concerned with her being alone night after night while he was away all week.

She could not hide the joy in her face at hearing his words and was unable to hide it as her smile puckered her lips. Her smile passed over to him.

"I can't tell you how happy I am to see you. It's been quite a while," he said.

"Yes. I've moved, you know, to my mother's home on St. Ann to take care of her. And she has since passed on." She nodded.

"I'm very sorry to hear of your loss. Please accept my sincerest sympathy."

"Thank you."

"I see you're alone on a Sunday."

"Yes, I'm alone."

"He never came back?"

"No, he hasn't."

"Rumors have it that he's left you."

"Yes, it appears he has, no thanks to your mother for the rumors, but I keep wondering if he'll return."

His face turned serious. "What do you really think?"

"The spirits tell me that he went back to Santo Domingo."

"It would appear so. Some say you've killed him, but I know that is not true."

"Yes, and who do you think started that rumor?"

"I'm so sorry that my mother has caused you so much misery. How can I make it up to you?"

"Well, we should not give her cause to gossip."

He looked away from her. "I see what you mean."

As they came upon her cottage, she stopped and said, "Good night."

He said, "Good night," meeting her eyes and continuing to look at her with admiration as they stood face to face.

"It would be a glorious night if you were to invite me in and allow me your company."

Feelings of excitement once again filled her. She felt uncertainty. She struggled with emotions she had not felt in a long time. Then, she felt frightened. "I think not," she let out in a breathtaking voice.

"I will respect that, Marie, as much as I want to rush to your lonesome heart and hold you in my arms and kiss you with a passion I've never known before. I will respect that you are a married woman."

Chapter 17

Many a night when Marie would come home to her empty cottage, she would find a woman waiting at her doorstep for advice, some for physical healing, some for personal healing. News had gotten around the city that Marie had a cure for everything, lost love, philandering husbands, cruel husbands, and runaway spouses.

She had just finished counseling a battered wife and retreated to her dining room to sit by the fire and rest before she warmed her food in the fireplace. She thought about the fact that she could re-unite husbands and wives, but she couldn't bring her husband back. Life had been hard this past year. She prayed for some solace in her lonely life.

A hearty knock brought her to her front door. Standing in front of her stood Christophe Glapion, lowering his head to peer into her sad eyes.

"Good evening again, madame. You look even sadder than the last time I called on you in your home. Are you alone?"

"Yes, I'm quite alone. Do come in, monsieur."

Her faintly amused smile reassured him that she did not object to his visit. She made him feel welcome without saying so. The fact that she now lived alone made him feel that her home was more open to him unlike the last time he paid her a visit.

He stepped inside and followed her past her prayer room. The large shadowy dining room felt cold as he watched her bend over to light a match and kindle the fire in the fireplace.

She rose and felt his stare. "Please sit." She pointed to a wooden chair at the head of the table. "Would you like some hot coffee?

"No, thank you, Marie. I'm quite fine. May I call you Marie?"

"Yes." She nodded and looked across the table at him, wondering the reason for his visit.

"My mother has had the croup. Your reputation for healing far surpasses even the doctors I know. Can you recommend something for her?"

"I would rather you bring your mother here so that I may look at her."

"I'm afraid that would be impossible. She would never come to your home, Marie."

"I see. Well, can you tell me a little more about her ailments?"

"She breathes heavily and has lost her voice. Marie, she's not the only reason for my visit. I have been wondering how you are doing all by yourself."

"Wait just one minute," she said as she took French leave and returned with a tiny, black sack filled with herbs. "These are for your mother. Have her brew them and take the tea three times a day. She will breathe better, and her voice will come back."

He rose and went to her. "Marie, you are the kindest woman in all this world. With all she has done to cause you unhappiness, you want to help her."

She looked up to him to find his shiny eyes glistening toward her. Twigs snapped and crackled in the fireplace as they looked into each other's eyes.

"It is not by accident that I met you on the street. I look for you."

"I have thought as much."

"I long to see you constantly. May I take you out so that we can spend time together?"

"But how can that be? People consider me a married woman even though my husband has been gone well over a year. And I don't think he will ever return. He thought I betrayed him when he found me in your arms."

"Marie, you are too beautiful not to be loved. You shouldn't live your life alone."

His face was inches from hers, and she could almost feel the heat from his body. She backed away. He moved in closer and finally held her in his arms. They both felt a warm satisfying feeling of relief. He looked into her eyes and realized that she held something dear for him, too.

She had stifled that feeling far too long. Her loneliness was too much to bear. She kissed him with the passion she had been holding in for months.

"My Marie. My Marie. I thought there was something there inside of you for me. I could feel it for a long time even though you denied it."

"Yes," she said. "I could feel it for you ever since I saw you looking so handsome in your uniform, walking proud and tall up Bayou Road."

He laughed, and they held each other for a long time.

She leaned onto him, and it finally settled in her brain that she loved him and wanted him.

"I love you, *mon chere*, and want to be with you." He kissed her passionately, the kiss he desired for a long time.

"I don't know if that could ever be. We come from different lines. That would never be accepted."

"Chere, do you think I care what other people think?"

"I don't know. What would your mother think? She hates me just for talking to you."

"We will not worry about others. Let us please ourselves. Do you love me, *mon chere?*

"Yes, I love you, Christophe." She felt her cheeks flush with excitement.

He lifted her up and carried her to her boudoir. Laying her on the bed, he kissed her and fondled her. "We must make ourselves happy and not worry about everyone else. You agree, don't you, *chere?"*

"Yes, but..."

"No buts, Marie. It is just you and I and our happiness. I want to make you happy more than anything in this world. I don't want to see you sad any more."

He unbuttoned her blouse and admired her light, bronzy skin. "I have never seen anything more beautiful."

He undressed her and stroked her body until she quivered, and he could wait no longer to make love to her. He undressed and engulfed her as she trembled in her passion. Kissing her and fondling her, she finally pulled him onto herself. "I can scarcely believe that I finally have your love and am in your body," he uttered. He thrilled that she moved her body to his thrusts, which excited him even more. She screamed in her passion, holding onto him so tightly, he could not hold back his orgasm. He tried to soothe her, tenderly stroking her body until she relaxed. She smiled up to him, and they held each other lovingly in a long embrace.

Christophe longed to be with Marie night after night and often spent the night with her. He did not tell his mother where he spent his nights, but Madame Glapion surmised that he spent them with Marie Laveau. She had noticed his curiosity whenever women brought up her name in their home. He never agreed with his mother that Marie did wicked things and practiced voodoo to an evil end. His disagreements did not go well with her. When she questioned him, he would say he has business at his notary office or he was about to sign a contract on an important real estate agreement and would rush off.

Chapter 18

When Marie was sure she loved Christophe within her soul, she went to Father Antoine and confessed her sin. She pounded loudly on Father Antoine's door. When he opened it and found her wiping her tears, he asked, "What's wrong, my child?"

"Father, will you hear my confession?"

"Of course. Come in."

Marie got down on her knees. "Father, I have committed adultery. And I lust for another man. We love each other!"

The priest did not have a look of pity but mercy, and she believed he would treat her as Jesus would and forgive and bless her. "Get off of your penitential knees. You have been put in this consequential position that is not your fault just as your station in life is not your doing. Your husband has been gone for a time now. We don't know if he has died on a journey, and no one has notified us. He may have gone back to Santo Domingo without intentions of returning."

"Yes. I want to re-marry, but I don't think that it is possible."

"If you can wait another year, I can declare you a widow, and you will be able to re-marry."

"Oh, Father, can you do that?" She held a look of doubt.

"Yes, God wants us all to be happy and lead a fruitful life. I will marry you and Christophe in the eyes of God in the church.

"I would forever be grateful. But then there is the other problem. He is a white man."

"Marie, I can solve the one problem, but you will have to solve the other one yourself. Many of my parishioners tell me how you have made their lives better. You will have to make your own life better. You are a free creole woman who serves God. People would approve of you to be a mistress to a white man, as a placee without the benefit of marriage, but not to be married to a white man. This community has failed you."

"Oh, thank you for that." Marie looked at him with grateful eyes. "No one has ever spoken to me in this way."

Pere Antoine helped Marie to her feet. "Child of God, just continue to do God's work, and He will smile on you."

"Yes, Father. Can you give me absolution?"

"I absolve thee of your sins. For your penance, say a rosary every night and continue your jail ministry with me. The prisoners appreciate the work we do."

"I will, Father. I promise to tell all of the people I heal to fill your church on holy days and the Sabbath."

They left his sparse room behind the cathedral to where Manvil was waiting for them with a large pot of catfish etouffee.

The three of them walked to the prison where the prisoners waited for them with their cup-filled hands outstretched through the bars. Manvil held the pot while Marie filled the prisoner's cups with etouffee. Father Antoine prayed with each prisoner and the one who was to be hung that day was led out of his cell and led to the outside where throngs of people anticipated the hanging. Marie walked to the opposite side and out the back door with Manvil. She didn't watch the hangings.

Evening came, and the shutters rattled in the wind, and she heard the rain pound down on the courtyard bricks. She felt chilled and went to her bed to get under her duvet and say her rosary.

That handsome man. He appears to love me—enough to marry me, and I love him. Oh, how I love that man! But I cannot marry him in my church before God because he is white. I can become his mistress, and my mother would approve and Father Antoine would continue to administer the Holy Eucharist to me out of his compassion for me and my station in life. I have to figure out a way to marry this man.

Chapter 19

"Yes, *mon cher*, he said he would declare me a widow, but we must wait until my mourning period ends."

"That is wonderful news! I am ecstatic," Christophe declared. "Then, we can be married."

"That does not solve our problem. It would not be legal."

Christophe sat pensively as if in deep thought. "Surely, there must be a way around this stupid law."

"I keep thinking, but there is no way." She shrugged.

He grinned toward her. "I think there is a way."

A question pulled at her face as she looked at him.

"If I were the same as you, there is no problem."

"No one would believe that you are the same as me."

"Of course, they would. My friends would back me up, especially if I documented on my baptismal certificate that I am a free quadroon and notarized it.

And you have so many friends beholden to you, they would vouch for you."

"And you would change your status to quadroon?"

"For you, *mon chere*, I would do anything."

Chapter 20

As Marie brushed Madame Colbert's hair in an upward motion and wrapped it in her usual bun, she noticed the sadness in her face. "You are upset, are you not, madame?"

"How did you know?"

"I could feel it."

"Oh, Mawree! My daughter is so sad, my heart breaks for her."

"Is she in love?"

"Yes. You knew, didn't you? The man she had been seeing is no longer calling on her. She introduced him to her best friend, and now he is courting her friend. She never leaves her room. I can't get her to come downstairs, not even for dinner. I purchased a new dress for her to go out in, and she refuses to wear it. Can you help her, Mawree?"

"I happen to have some ash tree leaves with me which has the power to mend a broken heart. If you brew these herbs for your daughter, it will mend her broken heart and make her happy and willing to meet another. Have her drink the tea twice a day."

"Oh, Mawree, I knew you'd have something for my daughter. Thank you," she said, as she took the herbs.

"May I go to her room and talk to her?"

"Oh, will you, Mawree? She likes you. She'll listen to you."

"May I come in, Clotilda?"

"Yes, Marie. Do enter."

Marie found Clotilda sitting at a rosewood desk, penning a letter. "Clotilda, your mother tells me that you are not happy."

"Oh, she shouldn't have bothered you with my problems."

"Clotilda, I meant to tell you something very personal for a time now, but I thought you already had someone very close to you. I know a very good man who has been having his eyes on you. He comes from a very good family, not far from here, and I know he would very much like to meet you. Do you think you could have it in your heart to meet him? He would be so happy.

"I don't know, Marie."

"Clotilde, I could fix your hair today so that it would look its best tomorrow, and your mother tells me she has purchased a beautiful dress for you and you will not wear it."

"I had no place to go to wear such a fine dress."

"Well, now you do. I know from this man's mother that he loves to go dancing, and I'm sure that he would love to dance with you."

"Is he an old widower. There's an older man who goes to my church who stares at me when I pray. I don't want a man twice my age."

"Oh, no, Clotilda. The man I want to introduce you to is a handsome, young man that any young woman would be proud to walk with—and dance with." Marie grinned broadly and nodded.

"If he's so good, why isn't he taken?"

"Many girls try to get his attention. I've seen it myself, but I think he has eyes for you. If I fix your hair today, may I invite him to your home for tea tomorrow?"

A long silence ensued. "You don't have anything better to do tomorrow, do you?" Marie looked into her eyes.

"Not really."

"Then, it's settled. Expect him tomorrow afternoon for tea at four."

Marie walked the six blocks in the American District to Madame Roudane's mansion. She remembered hearing Madame Roudane speaking of her son with great affection, hoping that he would get a wife good enough for him.

As she wrapped her hair around sticks, she approached the subject of her son. "And how is your handsome son, madame?"

"He's wonderful, as usual, Marie. He gets invited everywhere. I hardly get to see him."

"I have a wonderful young woman for him to meet."

"You do? And who is this wonderful woman you want my son to meet?"

"She is the daughter of the most successful lawyer in this city, madame. He is also an investor and they are very rich, and their daughter is exquisitely beautiful. I happen to know she is available."

"How do you know this family, Marie?"

"I do the mother's hair and the daughter's. The daughter's hair shines like gold. And she wears the most beautiful clothes I've ever seen. May we talk to your son about this lovely girl who has the best manners I have ever witnessed? I would like him to have tea with Clotilde tomorrow."

"Really, Marie. I'll ring for Carmona to ask my son to come to my salon. I believe he's in the library downstairs."

"Michael, do you have an engagement tomorrow afternoon?" Madame Roudane asked.

"I don't believe I'm busy tomorrow afternoon, Mother."

"Marie knows this family. The father is a successful attorney just blocks from here. What did you say their last name was, Marie?"

"Colbert."

"I think you should go and check them out. You're invited for tea tomorrow afternoon."

"Colbert. That name sounds familiar," Michael said.

"Maybe you already have met their daughter. What is the daughter's name, Marie?"

"Clotilda."

"Marie says she's a lovely girl. Go and meet her and see if you like her."

"Mother, do you really think this is necessary?"

"Michael, you have nothing to lose. Just an hour of your time. You're not obligated or anything. Then, come back and tell me what the family is like."

Chapter 21

A smiling black servant greeted Michael, as he entered the Colbert's mansion. "This way, monsieur. Mademoiselle will be with you shortly.

Before he turned to enter the drawing room, he couldn't help to notice the vision of white descending down the grand staircase.

He looked up to see a beautiful virginal-looking young lady with golden curls piled on top of her head in a flowing white dress. She stepped daintily one slow step at a time. Her long-lashed eyelids looked down. He couldn't tell if she was looking down at him or looking for the next stair, as she held her long dress up a bit so as not to trip, exposing her satin slippers. He longed for her to look at him.

The vision of this angelic creature mesmerized him. He couldn't move but stood still, watching her move down the stairs, flowing like a goddess.

When she reached the golden cypress floor, she greeted him with a feminine smile as their eyes met. He saw kindness in her face and thought her beautiful.

He cleared his throat. "I hope you don't think too brash of me, but Marie Laveau insisted that I meet you. I am Michael Roudane."

"Not at all. How do you do? I am Clotilda Colbert. How nice of you to accept our invitation to tea. Please come in." She led him out of the vestibule and into the drawing room.

Clotilda gestured for him to sit, but before he could, Madame Colbert entered the room with arms outstretched. "Hello, Michael. How wonderful of you to come to tea and meet us. We are practically neighbors. We should get to know one another." She shook his hand. "Please, sit and make yourself comfortable."

"This is my mother, Michael, as you've probably surmised," Clotilda said.

"Please, after you," Michael said, gesturing to the ladies.

Clotilda sat in a wing chair, and Michael chose a seat to best admire her."

Madame Colbert fixed a look at him and broke the silence. "So, Michael. What does your family do?"

"They are in the sugar cane business."

"And you?" she asked.

"I work in the family business."

Madame Colbert showed pleasure in her expression.

A servant entered with a large tray and set it on a serving cart. Madame Colbert asked Michael, "Do you prefer coffee or tea?"

"Coffee, please."

"Black or cream?"

"A spot of cream."

"Sugar?"

He raised his palm. The servant set his coffee on a small table next to him. He chose one small sweet from the tray offered to him.

He turned to Clotilda. "Do you like to dance, Clotilda?"

"Yes, I do, but I haven't lately."

"Well, we'll have to go dancing."

"That would be lovely," she said.

He felt an unexpected urge to see her again. The thought of being alone with her and holding her excited him. "I know it may be presumptuous of me to think you're free, but do you think we can go dancing tonight?"

She glanced at her mother, who gave her a wild stare, telling her not to refuse. "I think it can be arranged."

"Then, we'll go dancing tonight," he said with a wide grin.

Madame Colbert smiled in relief.

Chapter 22

Marie was happy to hear from both families that Clotilda and Michael were a match, and she was compensated by both the Colberts and the Roudanes. The families became friends. Marie saw how easy this was, gleaning information about their families from the women who were her hairdressing patrons. Now, Marie was in the matchmaking business.

When Father Antoine finally told Marie her proper mourning period had ended, and he could perform the wedding ceremony, Marie was ecstatic. "We will not announce banns, but will have a simple ceremony without pomp. I think it should be a candlelit midnight ceremony so as not to stir any gossip."

Father Antoine considered the gossip among the white people poisonous and did not want to fuel their tongues. He suffered ridicule for favoring the people of color. He baptized the children of the placees, administered the sacraments to them, and performed burials for prostitutes, concubines, and Freemasons, constantly defending them. On occasion, he had married people of mixed race forbidden by law over much controversy. He tried to make all of his parishioners feel like God loved them.

The white people who refused to recognize Marie's second marriage referred to her as the Widow Paris throughout her lifetime.

Marie only told her half-sister and Dehlia of her impending marriage, but the news traveled to Marie's cousins, nieces, nephews, and neighbors.

At midnight at St. Louis Cathedral, Christophe led Marie in her silk, plum-colored dress and matching tignon down the center aisle toward the candle-lit sanctuary where Father Antoine waited for them. Father Antoine almost choked with happiness for the couple.

"I know you have waited for this moment for a long time, and I'm most happy to join you in Holy Matrimony. It is better for you both to live Christian lives as one and continue to do good works, as you have, and raise children in the catholic faith then to live apart and be unhappy and lead a fruitless life. Therefore, I ask you, Christophe Duminy de Glapion, do you take this woman as your lawful wedded wife?"

"I do."

"I ask you, Marie Laveau, do you take this man as your lawful wedded husband?"

"I do."

"I now pronounce you man and wife."

They kissed and turned around to find Marie's family and neighbors celebrating with smiles and cheers. "Alleluia!" was heard coming from many mouths.

As Christophe and Marie walked past the communion rail, her family and friends held their arms out and embraced her in jubilation.

In the moonlight, the family walked together to Marie's cottage to celebrate, which was a complete surprise to Marie and Christophe. When they reached the cottage, many walked next door to Dehlia's home to retrieve the food and wine they stored in her home.

The fete began in Marie's home with Marie's favorite foods and music. They sang and danced until three in the morning, and would have stayed until dawn, but they knew Christophe and Marie had to be at work in the morning.

Moonlight slanted through her window, as she lay in bed. After he undressed, he joined her and felt delirious in his joy as he gazed down at her. "I love you so much, *mon chere*. I'm ecstatic. I've waited so long for you, but it was worth every minute to have you now as my wife."

"I'm happy too," she said and smiled up at him in a happy way he had never seen before.

"I thought they would never leave." He let out a long breath.

"Yes, I know. *Cher,* I didn't even know they were coming at such a late hour, but they said they had to celebrate our marriage."

The humid air outside was waxed with the sound of cicadas and the echoes of tom-toms droned from a party nearby. She smiled and pulled him to her naked body. His warm hands wrapped around her body and then moved up, feeling her soft light skin, traveling up to her neck and then down to her breasts. He felt their firmness, and she quivered. She kissed him as he rubbed her nipples fondly. She tried to speak words of love, her voice cracking, arching her back.

"Are you telling me you love me?" he asked.

"Yes, I love you."

"And I adore you," he said.

Her voice was sugared with welcome. "Come inside me," she invited.

He mounted her, looking into her glazed eyes. "I want you more than my life," he whispered.

The tom-toms outside sounded louder, as he entered her and he felt like he was moving to the rhythm of the pounding music. All around him, the pulsating music bounced, as he glided inside of her.

The cicadas high-pitched sound echoed throughout the night, its music spiraling into a high crescendo and blended to the rhythm of their lovemaking.

"What a glorious night!" he said in his passion with eyes closed shut. He glided in his lovemaking until he thought he could not continue, but his heart told him to wait for her, and then when she quieted, he fervently gave in to all the passion he felt.

"Was it good?" he asked.

"I am happy," she said.

Chapter 23

Madame Glapion throned in her home on Bayou Road with her plump daughter while everlastingly waiting for her son, Christophe. "Did you find out anything?" she asked Marie Dolores.

"Mama, sit down." Her daughter wiped the crumbs from her lips with her tongue.

"Why, what have you heard?" She squinted up at her daughter.

"Christophe has married the Widow Paris."

"What do you mean? How could he...?" she screamed in horror.

"He has declared himself a quadroon free man of color."

She pointed a finger at her daughter. "Don't you ever admit that horrendous thing to anyone! Don't you ever say those words again to me or to anyone," she screamed. "Oh, I can't believe those terrible words you uttered!" she wailed. "Oh, God! Oh, God, please tell me it's not true! Does he know what suicide he has committed?" She screamed in a high pitch, leaning over, as if in pain.

The pounding on the door stopped her wailing. With popping eyes toward her daughter, she quickly put her finger to her lips to warn her not to scandalize the family.

As Marie Dolores opened the door, Madame Glapion's next door neighbor rushed into the cottage as if there was an emergency. "Oh, Madame Glapion, what is the matter? Are you ailing?"

"Oh, it's just a pain I'm suffering in my breast. I must retreat to my bed."

"Oh, madame, are you sure you will be alright?"

"Yes, yes, I'll take my medicine, and the pain will go away. Thank you for your concern. Now, if you'll excuse me."

Madame Glapion went to her boudoir and tried to subdue her hysteria, repeating obscenities. "I think I'm going to faint," she screamed as she plopped in bed with her hand pressing her forehead.

Her daughter yelled from the front room, "Mama, I'm going to get your smelling salts."

When Marie Dolores appeared, she waved the smelling salts under her mother's nose, a custom she was in charge of.

"Oh, Mama, why do you let yourself get so upset? He's a grown man."

"Is this all my fault?" she rasped to her daughter.

"How is this your fault, Mama?"

"If I hadn't have told her husband that his wife was cavorting around town with my son, he wouldn't have left her in the first place, and she would probably still be married to him. Oh, am I being punished for that?"

Marie Dolores leaned over her mother's bed and fanned her with a huge palmetto fan to soothe her. "Oh, Mama, no! Don't blame yourself for this terrible humiliation to our family."

Madame Glapion sat up, suddenly feeling relieved, and questioned her daughter. "What's her bloodline? Who is her father? Oh, Yes, I know now. I met his wife. Remember her, Marie? That woman who said she owned the house next door and would evict her. I bet that black widow didn't even pay her rent. Well, I must have a talk with Madame Charles Laveau, the owner. The widow Paris's mother was not even married to her father. It will be very interesting to find out more details," she said with a smirk.

After a sigh, Marie Dolores said, "How will I be able to face my friends? We won't be able to hide this forever. They may think we're the same as him. Oh, Mama, what will we do?"

"I shall have you baptized Lawrence. Do you like that name?"

"Name?"

"Yes, I will call you Lawrence."

His broad smile opened his mouth to show a full set of white teeth. "Lawrence," he repeated. He repeated his name in reverence as if she presented him with a gift.

"Come and follow me," she said.

Marie quickly showed Lawrence her home, took him to the yard, and explained his duties. He would be in charge of planting the vegetables, hoeing the weeds, pruning the fruit trees, and keeping the coco-grass within the green lawn cut short so that her patrons could spread their blankets on it and have a more comfortable place to sit at her parties, and the Indian women could rest on the short lawn with their papooses. He would do the heavy work, lifting, and carrying the iron pots of etouffee to the prisoners in the jail with her because Marie was praying for a baby.

Chapter 26

The Friday night parties continued to make Marie's friends happy and took them away from the drudgeries of their hardworking lives. Marie stopped her dancing when she felt life in her body.

Christophe wanted her to work less, but Marie continued counseling those who came to her home. When she was summoned to a sick bed, she never hesitated to leave her home immediately.

Christophe occasionally visited his mother, Jeanne Sophie Lalande Ferrier Glapion, without Marie because Jeanne and her daughters did not accept Marie and looked down on the free people of color. His three snobbish sisters who had nothing to do with Marie had very little to live on compared to Marie who had a good income and thriving business. They would snub Marie when they saw her at the French Market. The colored circles that Marie and Christophe traveled in had better resources than his own white family whose fortune had dwindled by this time.

In late summer, Marie went into labor. Christophe ran for Martha, the midwife. Martha found Marie in the big walnut bed breathing heavily. She checked Marie to find she was close to delivery. "Oh, Marie. You are so brave. Why didn't you have me come sooner?"

"No need," she said.

"You don't need to be so brave. You can scream if you want."

"I don't feel a need to scream. But I do wish she would come soon. Martha, will you pray with me so that my baby will come soon? I don't know how long I can stand the pains." Marie stiffened and let out a whimper.

Martha took Marie's hand in hers and prayed. "Dear God, please bring Marie's dear child soon. She has waited long for her. Drink this." Martha put a cup to Marie's lips.

Marie took one swallow. "*Mon Dieu.* Martha, help me." She dug the heels of her hands into the mattress and let out a yelp. "Oh, God in heaven help me."

Martha checked to see how far she was dilated. "You're very close, Marie. It will be soon."

Marie let out a shrill. "*Mon Dieu, Mon Dieu*, why all this pain? I can't take it any more!"

Martha grabbed Marie's hands. "Squeeze my hands. Squeeze!"

"I can't. I can't do this any more."

"Sure you can. Squeeze my hands."

"No! Get away from me!" Marie rolled on her side.

"Push, Marie. Bear down."

Marie pulled away from Martha and pushed down with a loud grunt.

"Again."

Horror filled her face in agonizing pain as she pushed hard, and the baby's head appeared. Martha guided the infant into the world and cut the rubbery cord. "You were right, Marie, it's a girl, a beautiful girl."

Marie's face evened out in joy. She reached for the infant wrapped in a towel. "Hello, my sweet daughter. I shall name you Marie after your mother."

The baby did not cry and appeared to breathe unevenly. Marie could tell that the child had an abnormality. On the third day, Marie baptized her baby daughter Marie Louise Caroline before she died.

"Why does He hate me so much?" she shrieked. Marie's wild eyes stared at her confessor in the shabby room he lived in with his cot in the corner.

"He doesn't hate you, Marie," Father Antoine said, as he rose from his writing table.

"I do everything to help my neighbors, and He takes my children away from me. Two!" she said showing him two fingers. "He took away two of my babies!"

"Marie, God does not hate you. He never gives you a burden you can't handle."

"Hmphh. Well, I can't handle this. I can't. First, my Felicite, then my father and then my mother. Then, my husband leaves me to God knows where and now my baby. And I don't understand why."

"You are just going through a stage of grieving, my child. It shall pass."

"This is not a stage. I can't stand living any more. I want my child!"

"Your child is in heaven. She will wait for you."

"I don't want her to wait for me. I want her here with me."

"I will pray for you, Marie. And I ask you to pray, too. You help so many people who are sick. They wait for you. Look at the prisoners. They wait for you all the time to pray with them and give them food."

"I'm not going to that prison any more. I can't stand to see any more of their misery! Don't I have enough in my own life?"

"Marie, I will wait for you to come back and go to the prison with me, and I will pray for you."

"Don't wait for me, and don't bother to pray for me." In her tormented state, she ran out of the priest's sparse living quarters behind the cathedral.

Chapter 27

Marie's business increased as people came to her prayer room for advice on attracting a lover, bringing about a marriage, improving a business, returning a spouse, getting rid of a bad husband, or winning a case in court, which Marie was expert on with the help of her friend, the Chief of Police. Marie was also good at fortunetelling. Some wanted to know their future, and some came just to pray at her altar where a statue of Saint Mary and Saint Anthony stood next to pictures of saints, flowers, and candles.

Gris-gris became a big business for Marie as many came to her for them as well as herbs for their sicknesses. She had knowledge of the valuable healing qualities of indigenous herbs from her mother and grandmother. She made gris-gris consisting of roots and herbs, hot peppers, sugar and salt, flavorings, animal parts, graveyard dirt, gunpowder, pins and needles, dolls, candles, incense, holy water, and images of the saints, as she combined voodoo with folk Catholicism. Fifteen cents was her usual fee except for those who could obviously afford more.

Christophe acquired another slave for Marie to assist her in her business. The slave, Jude, would get up early and kill the snakes, chickens, and alligators. He would also fix the "dusts" and go with Marie to the American's homes and learn their personal problems from their servants and put cow's heads and black cats on their doorsteps. They would get scared and come running to Marie. She would tell them they were being hoodooed and charge them big money for a cure. She already knew about their affairs.

At her people's requests, she held voodoo services in her home. She became the uncontested queen of the voodoos with the most powerful gris-gris for both good and evil. People of color and white people paid high prices for her powerful spells.

A young, creole woman came to her home one day. "Madame, I am Mademoiselle Anna Bertreau. Can you give me something for my mother to stop her heavy flow?"

"Yes, I can. Please come in." Marie gestured for the woman to sit and returned with plantain leaves in a small, black sack and handed them to the young woman. "Tell your mother to brew four leaves in boiling water for ten minutes and drink the herbal tea three times a day. Her flow will subside."

The young woman reached for the bag and looked down. She did not make eye contact with Marie.

"You look very sad. Tell me what your problem is," Marie said.

Anna looked up to Marie. "I feel like a caged animal. My mother never lets me out of the house, except for today to get herbs for her. She has heard so much about you, madame, that she trusts you can help her. Yet, she doesn't trust me."

"Why does she not trust you?"

"Because she knows that I have a lover."

"And she doesn't want you to see your lover?"

"Yes."

"And why is that? Is he a free man of color?"

"No." She shook her head.

"Is he a married man?"

"No." Anna burst into tears. "Oh, I don't think you can help me."

"Do not doubt me, mademoiselle. I'm sure I can help you whatever your problem is. Tell me more."

"My mother caught us kissing."

Marie showed no reaction.

"I'm seventeen! Old enough to be long ago married."

"Yes. Then, why does she not approve?"

"Oh, I don't know if I can tell you." Again, she looked down as if in shame.

Marie sat next to Anna and took both of her hands into hers. "There is nothing you can't tell me, *chere*. I will help you. You are too young and beautiful not to be happy. This should be the best time in your life. Are you with child?"

"Oh, no. Nothing like that. I am so in love with her and I long to see her, but my mother forbids it."

Marie blinked in surprise. "Her?"

"Yes. I am in love with a beautiful woman who is twenty. My mother says it is a sin." She looked toward Marie. "See. I told you that you couldn't help me. It's hopeless."

"It is not hopeless. I will go with you and speak to your mother."

"Oh, please don't tell her that I told you about my love for Bernadette."

"I will not mention that at all, but after I speak with her, things will be better for you, and you will be happy."

"I would be forever grateful, madame. I don't understand how you will accomplish such a feat."

Anna, sad-eyed and nervous, walked with Marie down Orleans Street under the rusty balconies to the tune of a hurdy gurdy. Marie walked in her long swinging gait as if to the rhythm of the stringed instrument when her body slightly lifted. "When we get to your home, I want to speak to your mother alone."

"We are passing her home." Anna gazed upward to the second story of her lover's home. "Sometimes, Bernadette is in the window, hoping for a glance of me, but I do not see her."

"You will see her soon." Marie did not hesitate but continued in her steady gait without gazing up.

"Oh, madame, do you think it is possible?"

"I told you not to doubt me."

When they reached Anna's home, she introduced Marie to her mother. "Mother, this is Marie Laveau." She stretched her hand towards her mother. "My mother, Madame Bertreau."

Madame Bertreau humbled herself for Marie and bowed her head. "I am honored to meet you, Madame Laveau. Your reputation precedes you."

"You are most kind, madame. Those herbs are for you. Your daughter will prepare them for you as I have instructed." Marie turned to Anna and smiled. Anna left the room.

"Madame, I trust the herbal tea that your daughter is preparing for you will help you. Drink the tea three times a day until your flow subsides, which should be in the next few days. I must insist that you get off of your feet and rest in your bed."

"*Merci*, madame. I should feel most relieved."

"I must speak to you of Anna. She is suffering from a condition called melancholia. It must be taken care of right away or you will not have a daughter. She may waste away."

Madame Bertreau's eyes widened. "But how do you know that?"

"I see it in her eyes. They are yellowing, and if she does not get the proper care, it can be fatal."

Her eyes urged Marie to continue. "What do you suggest?"

"I suggest you send her to my home tomorrow for treatment, and after that, at least three times a week until she is well."

"What will you do for this melancholia?"

"I will have her rest in the sun on my yard and give her a formula I have made for this illness. I can see that she gets no sunshine whatsoever. She needs plenty of rest and sunshine, or she will waste away in death."

"Oh, by all means, madame, please treat her for this melancholia. I have noticed that she is not quite herself as of late."

"Then, I can expect to see her tomorrow by noon?"

"Yes, madame."

Anna appeared with the cup of herbal tea. "*Maman*, madame suggests you rest in bed. Let me help you to your boudoir."

"*Merci*, my Daughter, but I can find my way. Do attend to our guest. *Au revoir*, Madame Laveau."

"Your daughter will inform me of your progress, madame."

Anna led Marie to her front door. "Your mother has consented to allow you to my home three afternoons a week. Come tomorrow by noon and bring Bernadette with you. My home is your home," she whispered.

Chapter 28

Emotions welled up inside of her as Anna pounded on Bernadette's door. *Please, Bernadette, open the door. I am desperate.*

As Bernadette opened the door, Anna cried out to her, "Oh, Bernadette. I have some good news."

Bernadette pulled her inside. "What is it, Anna, *mon chere?*"

"The voodooienne, Marie Laveau, has convinced my mother that I need melancholia treatment. I go to her home for treatment three afternoons a week, and she has offered her home to us."

"Oh, my dear sweet Anna. Do you mean we can be together?" She held Anna close and kissed her.

"Yes, we should go to Marie Laveau's home now."

"I'll get a shawl." Bernadette rushed to another room.

As the two women excitedly hurried to the door, Anna stopped. "I think it would be unwise for us to be seen together on the streets. Someone may notice us and tell my mother we are together. I will go first. Wait a few minutes, Bernadette, and meet me at Marie Laveau's home at 152 Rue St. Ann.

"God speed, my sweet Anna."

"Oh, Marie, you were right. You can help me. May I call you Marie?"

"Yes, yes. I see that you're happy already. That was my intention all along—to make you happy."

"I can scarcely wait for Bernadette. Oh, it'll be so lovely to spend the afternoon with her. And I never thought my mother would let me out alone for an afternoon."

They heard a knock at the door. Anna could not contain herself and ran ahead of Marie. She opened the door and burst into laughter. "Come in, *mon chere*."

"Oh, what a pretty cottage you live in." Bernadette ignored the peeling paint of the adobe and stood with her eyes fastened on the banana trees and the herb garden. "And your herbs. What a feast."

"Yes." Marie laughed. "The herbs save the lives of many including mine. Please come in."

The women congregated in the prayer room. "I suggest we say a silent prayer to start out the afternoon. Let this begin a most happy time for the two of you."

Afterwards, Marie led the women through her home and onto her yard. "You may sit here and enjoy the scent of the jasmine while you get reacquainted. Then, if you tire of the sun and want some privacy, you may go to my boudoir. I will show you the way."

The two young women eyed each other and followed Marie, leading them to her boudoir. "You may rest here if you so desire and to make sure no one will intrude on your privacy, slip this chair under the door knob and no one will be able to come in. My parents did this to keep me out of this very same boudoir when I was a child."

"Madame, you are too good to us. How can we ever repay you?" Anna looked to Marie with appreciation.

"You can repay me by being happy."

Marie left the couple and went about her business, making gris-gris, not bothering to pay attention to their whereabouts. After a couple of hours, she crept silently to her boudoir to find the door closed.

Chapter 29

Marie was with child again. Christophe was very happy and took every precaution to protect Marie, since she had lost two of their children. He acquired a female slave, Virginie, to do the marketing and cooking.

He held her close in bed and felt the life in her body, touching it ever so gently. *"Mon chere*, I am so happy that we will have a child. You make my life worthwhile. This time, I will go for the midwife sooner."

"That had nothing to do with losing my Marie. Do not think that you are at fault."

"You should spend more time resting. You don't have to work so hard."

"I don't know how not to work, my husband. I come from a line of fever nurses and voodoo practitioners. It is in my blood to work. I must help my people."

"I know, my Sweet, but try to work less for me. I want this baby." He kissed her passionately but was afraid to put his body into hers for fear of hurting their child.

Two months later, Marie gave birth to a daughter and named her Marie Eucharist Heloise.

When Marie was doing "the work," she would go to her yard and place the statue of St. Anthony on his head. The children in the neighborhood would peek through the fence and shout, "Come and look. St. Anthony is standin' on his head!"

Marie Eucharist viewed this as her mother's routine and would go on playing.

Although Marie's home was filling with children, as she took in orphans from the streets to feed them, she never failed to nurse the sick when called to the aid of a fever victim. Virginie, her slave, freed Marie of household duties in order to make her gris-gris and nurse her patients as well as being a spiritual guide to many people. The slave, a stout woman with a pleasing personality, took care of the children to Marie's satisfaction when Marie was working.

The women of color were excellent fever nurses who refused to give out their recipes except to their children. They were often suspected of using their medicinal knowledge for deadly secret purposes.

Cholera and yellow fever became rampant in the city and believed to be caused by the swamp. Many tried to dissipate the bad air from the swamp and made conditions worse by burning animal skins, horns, hoofs, and tar. Many doctors made their patients worse by bleeding them, and administering emetics and purgatives that caused their deaths. The Afro-Creole fever nurses treated with herbal teas, cooling baths, massage, and nourishing broths and lost very few patients compared to their white counterparts.

The black fever nurses were furiously icing and massaging a room full of yellow fever patients in a dark slave-quarter room. Marie, who was two months pregnant, gagged at the stench, as she left the room to empty a bucket of black vomit and hoped to get a breath of fresh air outside. As she went down the rickety, wooden steps, a quadroon woman approached her.

"Marie, you must come right away."

"What is it? My child?" Marie felt frightened at the thought that her child may be sick with the yellow fever.

"It's Father Antoine. He's in his last hour. He has called for you, Marie."

"But I am needed here. I have to empty this."

The woman grabbed the bucket from Marie. "I will take your place. Go to him. It will soothe your heart to see him. I know how close you have been to him."

"Thank you, Zita."

Upon entering the room behind the cathedral, Marie came upon several women of color. The hum in the room created a mix of wailing and prayers. She spotted Father Antoine lying on his cot surrounded by the black women he had defended. She knelt at his bedside and felt the stone-cold feeling of his hand and wept.

An arm encircled her in her time of mourning. "Marie, there was nothing we could have done for him. It was his time. I was cleaning the church with him and he fell over, grasping his chest. I couldn't lift him, so I went for my husband and my slave and they carried him to his bed. He struggled to talk and said, "Go for Marie. Tell her I love her for the good things she has done for mankind. And he died."

"Oh, I should have been here for him," she cried. "I was so selfish, thinking only of myself."

"Marie, you are not selfish. You help everyone. Of all the women I know, you are the most generous. You even take care of children who are not your own."

"Someone must take care of them. Thank you for your kind words."

The women lamented together, grieving for their priest who fought against the racial laws that punished women of color and their children, embracing one another in their sorrow. Marie closed Father Antoine's eyes, and they proceeded to wash the monk's body and prepare it for viewing. They covered the altar in the cathedral on which his coffin rested with black drapes and flowing white feathers. Numerous candles lit the cathedral as the creoles viewed his body and mourned him. His memory merged with his patron saint, St. Anthony of Padua.

Chapter 30

A young woman appeared at Marie's front door one day in tears.

"What in God's name is the matter?" Marie asked. "Please, come in."

The young woman walked into the prayer room and spied the altar with the statue of St. Mary and several pictures of the saints. "I've heard that you're very spiritual and that you help everyone in dire situations. And I am in a dire situation."

"Yes. Tell me your situation. And your name?" They sat next to each other.

"I'm Liza, madame. I was forced into a loveless marriage by my parents recently. It was because his family has money that could help my father's business. The man I am married to is loathsome. I cannot stand to be with him another minute. He pays me no mind except to push his way into me in bed. He yells at me to tears. He keeps a whip in our boudoir and threatens he will use it on me if I don't do everything he says. He keeps me from seeing my mother and father. And he looks at me violently when he loses his temper as if he's going to strike me, waving his fist at me. I am afraid of his temper. It's only a matter of time that he will beat me. He's threatened that he will, if I don't listen to him. I fear he may impregnate me. I don't want his child. I must leave him."

"I see. Do you know where you will go?"

"I decided to take the boat upriver on Friday morning."

"Then, you've decided what you want to do."

Liza burst into tears. "I don't want to go without him."

"Who?"

"I am in love with a young man, Richard. We planned on marrying. When I told him I was being forced into marrying my parents' choice for a husband, he was devastated."

"I understand."

"I want to let Richard know I am leaving the city. He tends bar at The Old Decatur Tavern. I cannot go there, or word will get to my husband that I went to the tavern to see Richard. Can you take a letter to him, please?" She looked up to Marie with tearful eyes.

"How will I know him?"

"He is young and handsome. We are both seventeen. His eyes are blue and he has wavy, brown hair. He would probably be behind the bar. If you could get a note from him, that would be splendid."

"I will go to the tavern tomorrow and encourage a note from him. Come back to me the day after tomorrow."

"Oh, thank you madame. I didn't know who to turn to. I'm not allowed to go to my mother. My friends have told me about you, and they were right." Her brow furrowed as she looked at Marie. "But I hope he will not impregnate me."

"I will give you something. It is an herb that will prevent you from conceiving. Brew it yourself. Don't trust anyone else to do it. Place two leaves in boiling water and brew them for ten minutes. Drink it twice a day in private." Marie left the room and returned with a little cloth bag containing the herbs and handed it to Liza.

"Thank you, madame. I can hardly wait until the day after tomorrow. I know I won't sleep a wink until then."

"Let us pray that you will attain happiness and serve God."

The women knelt before Marie's altar and recited The Hail Mary and then prayed to St. Rita, the patron saint of battered wives. "Please, St. Rita, intercede for God's child, Liza. Let no harm come to her." And they prayed to the spirits for Liza's journey to a new life.

Marie made her way to Decatur Street past the taverns and sailors, giving her the eye. Her black eyes were as black and bright as a mouse, anticipating the wild stares but continuing on without a return look to accomplish her task at hand.

When she came into the tavern, men stopped talking to turn to look at her with admiration. She walked past the men at the bar until she spotted Richard shoving a stein toward a sailor.

He stopped talking mid sentence when he spotted Marie. They locked eyes. "May I speak to you, Richard?"

He walked to the end of the bar to meet her. "I have a letter for you from Liza."

His lips parted into a broad smile. She handed him the letter. He anxiously took it and read it.

Dear Richard,

I do not love my husband. I am leaving him to take boat 14 at seven a.m. on Friday. I may go to St. Louis where I have an aunt who will harbor me. I love you.

Liza

Richard put his hand to his forehead, looking rather shocked. He stood speechless, holding the letter.

Marie waited for a reply to no avail. "Do you have an answer?"

"An answer?" He looked dazed.

"Yes. I know she would love a reply."

"What would I say?"

"That you love her, too. You love her, don't you?"

"Yes, I love her. But she's married."

"Hasn't she told you that her parents forced her to marry this man she doesn't love? Hasn't she told you she does not love him but that she loves you?"

"Uh-huh." He looked dumbfounded, his mouth open.

"She wants to start a new life away from New Orleans. I'm sure she would want to have a life with you."

"She would?" He looked surprised.

"You said that you love her, didn't you?"

"Yes, I love Liza."

"And she said she loves you."

He stood, thinking in a daze. Shouts from the sailors woke him.

"Hey, gid yersef over here, boy, and gid us some brew." The old sailor pounded on the bar.

"Do you want to see her again?" Marie asked.

"Yes, I do!"

"Then, tell her that you'll meet her at the boat next Friday at seven a.m. unless you don't want to see her ever again."

"Madame, I don't have a writing implement with me. Can you please tell her that I will meet her at boat fourteen on Friday at seven a.m. with my bags. And tell her that I love her."

"I will do that, Richard. Give me her letter so that no one else gets their hands on it."

Marie felt satisfied that her mission was accomplished. As she walked out of the noisy tavern, a man followed her and stopped to admire her. Marie turned to the man with a wild stare as if to say, "Stop it. Go away or I'll put an evil spell on you." The man listened to her evil eye and turned away.

Liza came to Marie's cottage early on Wednesday morning before Marie had her morning coffee. "Come and sit with me," Marie invited, as she led Liza to her dining table. "Did you have coffee?"

"No, I haven't. I could hardly wait to see you."

"Virginie, serve us coffee and bring us some pain perdu from that hot bread you just baked. We will have breakfast."

Virginie poured coffee into cups at the table and brought cream and butter with her pain perdu.

"Leave us, Virginie. Go to the garden and pick some fresh vegetables." Marie knew better than the white creole women who thought their servants invisible and that their servants didn't hear all of the gossip going on in the family, or that their servants did not understand French. Marie did not want Virginie to hear Liza's plans to run away and possibly get the news about the neighborhood and to Liza's parents and husband.

Before Liza could take a bite, she asked. "Do you have a note for me, madame?" Her large eyes were almost watery as they stared at Marie.

"No, but he told me to tell you that he will meet you at boat 14 on Friday at seven a.m. with his bags. And that he loves you."

"Oh, I can hardly believe my ears." She jumped up and hugged Marie.

"Now, *chere*, can you keep a secret?" Marie looked into her eyes.

"Yes, I believe I can."

"Secret your feelings. Take every precaution not to spoil this. Do not act any different with your husband or your parents. Don't act happy all of a sudden or they will wonder what change is taking place. Even if you don't sleep, lie still. And are you drinking the tea?"

"Yes, madame."

"Good. Now, I'm going to burn your letter in the fire so that no one puts their hands on it including servants. When you go home, act natural. Don't smile and don't cry. Just be plain and ordinary." Marie placed Liza's letter in the fire.

Liza handed Marie two twenty-five cent pieces.

"Thank you, *chere*. Now, let's go into the prayer room and pray for a safe trip for you and Richard. I will pray that the spirits will guide you. And to St. Rita to protect you."

Chapter 31

Christophe's idolatry of Marie deepened with each child that she gave him. They were expecting another child. Unlike Jacques, he supported her voodoo work. He played the guitar for Marie in the evenings when she didn't have patrons coming to her home for council. He often massaged her back in the privacy of their boudoir. When Marie wasn't tired, he would make love to her upon opening the windows to allow the beautiful scents of the lime trees and the jasmine vines to waft in the air.

This evening, he helped her prepare for a voodoo service. They spread a white tablecloth upon the floor in the prayer room, and carefully placed offerings of herbs, fruit, bottles of rum, flowers, candles, coins, congri (rice and peas) and red peppers on it. They placed candles in the four corners of the room and on the altar and lit them.

Soon, many white-garbed black women, white kerchieves wrapped around their heads, barefooted, entered Marie's home with food offerings. They placed food on the altar and took food to Marie's dining room for after services. Black men with African drums, stringed instruments, jawbones, and triangles walked in. More white women than black attended. A few young, black singers came in, smiling broadly.

Most of the voodooists were also Catholics and attended mass in the Roman Catholic Church on Sundays.

Marie noticed a newcomer. Madame Villere was guiding her slave, Zelda, into the room as if leading a blind person.

"Good evening," Marie greeted.

"I brought Zelda. Her husband insisted I bring her to you. Can you help her? She hasn't slept or eaten since her boy…"

Zelda's lifeless face took on the face of a zombie. Puffiness appeared under her staring eyes that focused on nothing, seeing nothing, hearing nothing, everyone appearing dead all around her.

"Yes, of course. Sit here, Zelda." Marie offered Zelda a chair against the wall and guided her onto it. A few chairs lined the walls for the elderly and crippled.

Grasping Madame Villere's hand with deepest sincerity, she said, "I'm glad that you came and brought Zelda. I will help her. Come and join the women."

Marie walked to the altar and led the prayers. "Hail Mary, full of grace! The Lord is with thee;" And then The Apostle's Creed. "I believe in God the Father Almighty, Creator of heaven and earth;" The worshippers joined her in prayer. She looked upon the people and said, "Let us thank Nana Baluku for the full moon tonight enlightening our lives.

We pray to the Black Madonna, virgin of the angels, for solace, protection, fertility, the will to give up one's sorrows, and for protection of mothers and children. Let us pray for Zelda, a mother who brought four sons into this world, and pray to the Black Madonna that she heals her in her time of grieving."

A chant burst from her mouth, as the people followed her around the room, circling the tablecloth on the floor, as she shook a beaded rattle to the rhythm of a dance, and the men beat their African drums and played their string instruments. They sang, shuffling with more movement of the hips than of the feet, backward and forward, while chanting.

> Atibon Legba Open the gate for me
> Papa Legba Open the gate for me
> Open the gate that I can enter
> God Legba Open the gate for me

They danced around the room in circular fashion. The chanting became louder. The sound of the rattle became more intense. The chanting went on faster and faster as the worshippers danced frantically until one male worshipper fell to the floor, shaking his body uncontrollably. A woman fell to the floor, weeping and falling into a trance.

Some howled and chanted as they gyrated in and out of the circle. Some fell to their knees and cried. "Papa Legba! Papa Legba!"

And then the chanting stopped. People were catching their breaths. Some worshippers went to pick the man and woman off the floor who seemed to come out of a deep sleep, not remembering how they got on the floor. Two women came with water to revive the frenzied worshippers.

Two black boys began singing a hymn and the mood changed. Many worshippers sat on the floor, resting and listening to the hypnotic hymn.

One young, black boy sang a solo at the request of many of the worshippers. His sweet soprano voice had not yet changed, and people loved to hear him.

Marie said a blessing of the food, and people went up for food and drink in her dining room as a young boy played accordion music.

After several more people sang, some thanked Marie for the spiritual evening and left the cottage, leaving a donation in the basket at the door.

Marie walked up to Madame Villere. "I want you to leave Zelda with me. I will help her through her time of mourning. The rest in my home will help her in her time of grief."

Madame Villere looked into Marie's eyes with surprise. "Do you honestly want me to leave her with you?"

"Yes. The least I can do is offer her my home to rest in and nurse her as best as I can."

"Thank you, Marie Laveau. What I've heard of you is true.

Marie guided Zelda to a small room, carrying a candlestick. Against the wall stood a raised, wooden platform covered with cotton padding in lieu of a mattress for reasons of economy.

"Lie down here, Zelda."

Zelda stood without emotion, hanging onto her shawl.

Marie helped her onto the bed. "Wait here. I'll get you a quilt."

She returned with a cup of chamomile tea and a quilt. Covering Zelda with the quilt, she saw her shiny eyes staring out into space. Raising Zelda to a sitting position, she put the teacup to her lips. Zelda responded stoically.

Marie lay her down and glided lavender leaves and hawthorn leaves about her face, back and forth, then sang to her peacefully.

Zelda appeared to be relaxing, the frown lines in her forehead slightly fading. When offered the tea again, she took small sips at a time.

Marie removed her blouse and turned her over and massaged her back with a balm of valerian and lobelia. When she turned her over on her back, she saw an improvement. Her frown lines were diminishing and for the first time, she looked into Marie's eyes. "You look better. Can you speak to me?"

Zelda's lips parted in a struggle. "I lost my Ben. My little boy."

"I know, Zelda. I know the pain." Marie closed her eyes, remembering her own anguish. "I lost three babies." She took Zelda's hand and gripped it. Zelda squeezed back. Marie began to sing a hymn to a more relaxed Zelda.

"Tell me 'bout yer babies," Zelda rasped.

"Well, I had my little Felicite when I was just a mere sixteen years old. She was the prettiest baby girl you could ever lay your eyes on. She died at nine months old in her little basket like some babies do. Then, my little Marie died at a few days old. She had a hard time breathing. And my little Francois. Oh, the pain of losing my first little boy. I can hardly speak of it."

Zelda consoled Marie. "You poor mama. You know just how I feel. Only you, who lost babies, knows the pain of a mama like me."

Marie rubbed oil she infused with jasmine and kava kava to Zelda's forehead to promote relaxation and help Zelda get a good night's sleep.

To get more comfortable, Zelda turned on her side. Marie sang a lullaby, stroking her back until the brokenhearted slave-woman fell into a deep sleep, snoring wildly.

As the birds chirped throughout the morning, Marie continuously found Zelda asleep. At noon, she checked on her to find Zelda's eyes squinting up at her.

Zelda rubbed her eyes and asked, "Where am I?"

"You're in my home."

"Why am I here?"

"You need to rest yourself and now you need to eat." Marie sat on the makeshift bed and offered Zelda a spoonful of coush coush (cornmeal mush mixed with eggs.)

Zelda accepted the mush as Marie fed her. The first positive words came from her mouth. "This tastes good."

"Here, you want some molasses on it?" Marie felt pleased that Zelda ate with zest.

Zelda nodded.

Marie dipped a spoonful of molasses into the mush and fed it to her.

"What time is it?" Zelda asked.

"Past noon."

"Oh mah Gawd. I never slept this late in ma whole life. Didn' sleep a night since…" A tear ran down her black cheek, as she suddenly remembered her little boy was gone. She gulped the last spoonful. "I gotta go. Madame Villere will be furious at me for sleepin' so long."

"You just lie right down. You're not going anywhere. Madame brought you here so you could rest and get well. She trusted me to take care of you. Now, lie yourself down, and I'll get you a cup of coffee and a piece of Virginie's home made bread."

Returning with coffee and bread, Marie found Zelda asleep. She covered her with a quilt and left the coffee and bread on the night table.

❧

The next day, Marie bathed Zelda in a bath of linden flowers, chamomile flowers, lemon balm herb, and lavender flowers. She rubbed her back with her homemade lavender soap until her body felt completely relaxed. Zelda leaned back in the big tub with her eyes closed. Marie dressed her and led her to sit in her yard to get some sunshine. At lunchtime, she served Zelda catfish and fresh vegetables.

"Now, you have to eat, *chere,* to get your strength back." Marie fed Zelda her first taste of the fish.

"Mmmm. What is it?" She looked at Marie with appreciation.

"It's catfish."

She took a tiny bite.

"Eat it all up now. And here's your tea." She pointed to the tall glass of chamomile-lime tea.

When Marie returned, she found the catfish and vegetables had not been eaten, and Zelda had fallen fast asleep in the afternoon sunshine amid the scent of the jasmine flowers and elderflowers.

By the fifth day, Zelda became more responsive to Marie's treatment of herbs and rest. As Marie brought Zelda her morning herbal tea, she decided to get Zelda to talk. "Tell me about your dear son, Zelda. What did he like to do?"

Zelda's face lost its sadness, and her eyes sparkled for the first time. "Oh, he all the time helped me. When we went to market, he helped me carry the bags. When I was peelin' and cuttin' the vegetables, he was peelin' and cuttin' with me. He was like my right hand. Oh, I don't know how I can go on without him. Ya know, they sometimes take yer babies away from you and sell 'em after they're 'bout ten years old. I asked Madame Villere if she'd keep my babies and not sell 'em. And I told her how attached I was to my little Ben, like skin on a peach. She promised me she'd never sell my babies."

"That was very good of Madame Villere. She's a very good woman."

"Yes, but that didn't do me no good. My Ben. He's gone." Zelda thundered in wailing tears that sounded like they finally broke through a stone wall.

Marie reached for her quivering body and held her until the sound of her wailing broke.

"Oh, you so good to me, madame, and I so much trouble to you, you a mama who lost three babies."

"You're no trouble to me. I help you, and you're helping me, too."

"I don't know if I'm helping you, but I feel better than when I came here."

"That's what I wanted. Let's go and thank the spirits for mending you. I also want to cleanse your soul."

At the prayer room, Marie placed a bottle of brandy and herbs upon the altar and lit the candles. She took dried sage leaves and dried sweet grass and placed them in a clay pot and lit a match to the herbs. She waved her hands upward to promote smoke as the burning leaves permeated the room with an aroma only these leaves could create. As she waved her arms upward to arouse the smoke, she started to pray.

"Hail Mary full of grace…." And "I believe in God the Father Almighty Creator of heaven and earth…"

Zelda joined Marie in the prayers as the aroma-filled smoke filled the room. Then, to Legba, intermediary between the real world and the spiritual world.

> Antibon Legba Open the gate for me
> Papa Legba Open the gate for me
> Open the gate that I can enter
> God Legba Open the gate for me

"We honor those who have passed before us and thank thee for mending my sister, Zelda, in her time of grief. We pray that her son, Ben, will welcome her when she passes from this world to the spiritual world and in the meantime console her and take away the sorrow that she feels. Cleanse her soul."

Smoke wafted in the prayer room as Marie waved the smoke in Zelda's direction. Zelda closed her eyes in prayer to the spirits and thanked them silently for this time with Marie.

Marie sang a hymn as Zelda knelt and let out the tears she had left in her. Marie knelt next to Zelda and meditated.

When they left the prayer room, they both felt exhilarated. Marie was happy to see all the lines of sadness had left Zelda's face. Marie led Zelda to the dining room. "You haven't eaten yet today. I pray that you have an appetite."

"Oh, I remember that catfish you once served me. I feel like I can eat a whole fish."

"I'll have Virginie cook one up for you with some eggplants, and I've picked some thimbleberries for you. The spirits have answered my prayers!"

Chapter 32

Marie bore another baby girl she named Marie Philomene. Since she already had a half-sister on her mother's side, Marie Louise, a half-sister on her father's side, Marie Dolores, and a daughter named Marie Heloise Eucharist, people called her Philomene to avoid confusion.

She carried her baby as the Indian women carried their papooses in front of her waist to be close to her. She kept Philomene wrapped around her body as she prepared gris gris and counseled her patrons.

Virginie eyed Marie nursing her baby, as she mixed shrimp etouffee in a big pot and hung it above the fireplace. "You sure do love that baby, madame. I never seen a mama hang onto a baby as much as you."

"Yes, I adore her." Marie looked up to Virginie. "Have you had babies?"

"I had five." Virginie's face turned into sad contemplation. "They took 'em all away from me includin' my baby, Sissy. She was only 'bout six when they pulled her away from me. I remember she screamed and cried, but it didn't do no good. They sold her to another family even though by law they shouldna taken such a young child away from her mammy."

"She'd be 'bout fourteen now, wouldn't she?" Marie touched Virginie gently on her arm.

Virginie nodded with a frown.

"Have you any idea where she went?"

"Latest I heard she's livin' with a family in the Faubourg Treme on Roman near Dumaine. I miss her so much because she's my baby just like you can't stand it when you're away from your baby."

Marie looked across the room at Virginie's suffering eyes. "I know friends who live on Roman. "I'll look for her and find her for you."

A light swooped across Virginie's face as she stared at Marie. "You could do that?"

"Of course. I've worked in that area many times. I'll bring her to you, Virginie."

Relief passed over her face as she stepped back and fanned herself with her large palms. "I can't believe my ears," she said with a quivering chin.

Patting her baby's back, Marie said, "I can leave as soon as Philomene falls asleep. "I'll put her down in my boudoir. I want you to come to my boudoir if she cries and hold her and pat her back. You may not take her to the cookhouse and cook while you hold her. And don't take her in the dining room near the fireplace and the hot pots on the hearth while you warm food. You are not allowed to hold her and warm food at the same time. Do you understand?"

"Yes, madame. I know how much you love this baby, and I won't let anything happen to this child.

Marie walked to the Treme Faubourg and called on a co-worker, Mama Antoine, who sometimes held the voodoo services in her home on Dumaine near Roman Street.

"Mama Antoine, I have a favor to ask of you."

"Marie! Funny to hear you asking me for a favor."

"Do you know a young slave girl called Sissy who lives near you?"

"Yes, I've seen her about."

"I want to take her to her mother, Virginie, my slave. Can you show me where she lives?"

"Yes. I'll take you to her. She lives with the Maraist family. They have many children."

The two mambos walked to Roman Street where Mama Antoine pointed out the home where Sissy lived. Marie knocked on the door.

A slave answered with an inquiring look.

"I have come to speak to Madame Maraist. Tell her Madame Marie Laveau has come to talk to her."

Madame Maraist appeared, looking quite surprised to see two women of color at her door.

"I am Marie Laveau. I've come to talk to you about your slave, Sissy."

"Has she done something wrong?" Madame Maraist widened her eyes in surprise.

"No, it's nothing like that. Her mother is my slave. The child was taken away from her mother at such a young age, I want to unite them."

"Oh, that's not possible. We paid a good price for her."

"I am willing to pay an even better price."

"You see, I really need Sissy. I have a very large family, and Sissy helps to take care of the children."

"You would be able to buy two slaves with what I would pay you."

"It's not entirely my decision to make. I would have to discuss this with my husband."

"May I come in and discuss this with you and your husband?"

"What did you say your name is?"

"Marie Laveau."

She put her finger to her chin. "I know now. I've read your name in The Picayune. You've saved many from the yellow fever."

Marie nodded.

"Please come in."

Mama Antoine started to walk away. "I'll leave you now to your business, Marie. Come and visit me soon."

Marie was led to a sitting room where she waited for Monsieur Maraist. When he entered, he immediately recognized Marie from a consultation he went to her for, but did not admit this to his wife.

"Madame, it's my pleasure to meet you. How can we help you?"

Marie did not admit recognition either. "I am interested in purchasing your slave, Sissy."

"We are quite fond of Sissy as she looks after our large brood. My wife would be lost without her."

"Yes, she has told me that. I am willing to pay a handsome price for her. You would be able to replace her twofold."

"What would that price be?"

"Six hundred American dollars."

Monsieur Maraist hid his thoughts and rubbed his goatee. "Why are you so interested in owning this young girl? Why not buy another?"

"She was separated from her mother, my slave, Virginie, when she was but six years old. As you well know, that is not legal or moral to separate a child from her parent. As a mother, I know the pain of separation, not from someone purchasing my child but by death of three children." She looked toward Madame Maraist. "Certainly, madame, you as a mother understand how you would feel if someone took your child never to see her again. And I think the child must miss her mother and her siblings."

Madame Maraist looked to her husband. The play on her face told him that for the first time she felt sympathy for Sissy. Before, she felt Sissy lucky to be in her family, to be able to be with her lovely children, to have enough good food to eat, but now after hearing Marie put it another way, her heart had changed.

He thought she looked at him for permission to let Sissy go. *"Chere,* what do you think?"

"I don't know. Now, she's like my child. I've had her for eight years."

"You see how it feels to have someone taken away from you. I live in the *Vieux Carre*, and you may feel free to come to my home and see Sissy and her mother, Virginie, any time you want. And your children are welcome, too."

"How gracious of you," Madame Maraist said.

"If we were to decide to let Sissy go, we would need time to replace her," Monsieur Maraist said.

"My husband is a notary and deals in real estate and slave trading. He would be most happy to find the best slave or slaves to replace Sissy. He could take you tomorrow."

"That would help." Monsieur Maraist looked pensive, still not sure whether to make a decision.

"I must tell you that with the large family that you have, there will be a time when you will need a nurse. If that time comes, I will be at your doorstep to help you. My mother and grandmother were fever nurses, and I have followed in their footsteps."

"She is the one I told you about, *cher*. The one I read about in The Picayune who has saved many from the yellow fever," Madame Maraist said.

"Oh, yes, my dear," pretending he did not know Marie, but he full well knew of her powers and her talent as a fever nurse.

A black servant hurried into the room. "Madame, the child, Willie, is hot. His nose bleeds."

"Oh, no!" Madame Maraist turned to Marie. "Will you help us?"

Marie rose without hesitation and followed Madame and monsieur through rooms until they came to a stairwell and took steps to a room where a young boy lay in bed.

Immediately, Marie took over by raising the boy's back, allowing the blood to flow. "Bring rags," she said.

Monsieur Maraist left the room and summoned a servant.

Marie felt the boy's forehead and looked into his eyes.

Watching the blood raging from her son's nose, Madame Maraist looked on in desperation. "Is it the yellow fever?"

The servant came in with rags and handed them to Marie, who held them to the boy's nose.

"How long has he had the fever?" Marie asked.

"I only feel him hot today and he cough," the servant said.

"It's good that he only started to be hot today." Marie reached into the slit of her skirt into a pocket with a string tied around her waist and pulled out dried herbal leaves. "Take these leaves and boil them in boiling water for ten minutes. Bring the tea back to me."

Monsieur Maraist strode to his wife, putting his arm around her shoulder to console her. "What is it, madame? Is it the fever?"

I do not see yellow in his eyes or his skin. I do not think it is yellow fever, but he does have a fever. I will treat the fever with herbal tea. I must ask you to bring cold rags soaked in cold water and we will apply them to the boy." Marie looked around the room to see several children's beds in the room. "I must tell you to keep your other children out of the room. They must sleep elsewhere. This is most likely influenza and very contagious, even for you. Do not touch your boy or kiss him."

"What about you?" Monsieur Maraist asked.

"I have a natural immunity. It is a gift I am grateful for."

The servant entered with the cold, wet rags and handed them to Marie. "Leave me now. I will take care of him."

The servant left the room, while the parents lingered and watched Marie apply the cold rags to the boy's body. The boy screamed in pain.

"Oh, my boy, Willie!" Madame Maraist cried.

Marie looked back at them. "Leave us."

The parents left the room with hesitation.

Marie fed Willie sips of herbal tea and cooled him down with cold rags. After three hours, she left the room to find Madame Maraist in the hall. "Madame, my breasts have filled with milk. I must go to feed my baby. I will be back very early in the morning."

"Is there anything we can do?

"If the boy screams of heat and pain in the head, you may apply the cold rags, but be careful not to touch his skin or the water or blood from his nose. Just touch him with rags. He is sleeping for now, and maybe he will sleep for a while until I return."

An eyelash of a moon hung in the dark, starless night, as a servant drove Marie home where she immediately washed her body down with her disinfectant soap and wrapped herself in a warm blanket. She took a crying Philomene from Virginie's arms and nursed the infant.

"I can hardly wait to ask you. Did you see Sissy?" Virginie asked.

"I didn't see her, Virginie, but I feel sure they will sell her to me. Right now, I am nursing their young son who has a fever."

"Oh, my Gawd. Is it the yellow fever?"

"No, he has a fever but it is not the yellow fever."

"Thank goodness. I want for you to get Sissy out of that house where they have the fever."

A carriage waited for Marie the next morning to take her to the Maraists. She found the boy, Willie, coughing with fever. She summoned more herbal tea and cold rags. She tirelessly cooled the boy with the rags and fed him sips of tea for three hours. The boy's fever was going down, and she retreated to her home to nurse her baby. Her cleansing ritual of her body continued every four hours for three days so as not to bring the fever to Philomene. Upon the evening of the third day, the boy no longer had a fever.

The parents retreated to Willie's bedroom, feeling delighted that they could talk to him and embrace him. "We are so delighted, Madame Marie. How can we ever repay you for our son?" Madame Maraist asked.

"You can let me take Sissy to her mother. Her mother is waiting for her."

"I think we owe it to you," Monsieur Maraist said. "We will bring Sissy to you now."

Marie rested in a chair waiting for Sissy. A young teen-aged girl, looking frightened, entered the bedroom.

"Come here, Sissy. Don't be afraid. I won't hurt you."

"Are you going to take me away?" Fear filled her voice.

"I'm going to take you to your mother. She has been waiting for you for a long time."

"Where is she?"

"She lives with me."

"I don't want to leave the children," Sissy cried.

"But your mama is crying for you. I hear her cry for you every night."

"Why has she waited so long to find me?"

"She did not know where you were. Then, she heard that you lived in Treme on Roman Street near Dumaine. I have a friend in this area who led me to you."

"I don't know." The girl trembled, pinching her fingers together.

"You don't have to be afraid. I never beat my servants. I treat them well and feed them well. My servants never get sick. Don't you want to see your mama?"

"Yes, I do want to see my mama. I cried for her, too."

"Then, just come with me, child, and you will meet your mama. Do you like little babies?"

"I love babies." The first smile showed on Sissy's lips.

"Well, I have a little baby girl, not even six weeks old. Do you want to see her?"

Sissy nodded reluctantly, as Marie led her out of the room. She looked back towards the door as if she wanted to run back in.

The driver waited outside for them and drove Marie and Sissy to the St. Ann Street cottage amid Sissy's muffled cries.

"Don't be so sad. My home is a happy place. It is always filled with children. The neighborhood children love to come to my place. You'll see."

Virginie quivered in anticipation of seeing her daughter again. She kept telling herself not to feel so happy for fear of great disappointment in case Sissy's owners would not release her and Marie would have to come home without her. She prayed with a lump in her throat that her daughter would return to her.

When Marie and Sissy entered the large dining room, Virginie was standing in front of the fireplace with her hands to the sides of her face as if she saw a vision. "Is that really you, my baby?" She held her arms out to her daughter.

Virginie saw hesitation in her daughter as if trying to recognize the lines in her mother's aging face. She called out to her. "Come to your mama, Sissy, my baby."

Sissy recognized her mother's voice and then as she came closer, she looked into her mother's eyes.

Sissy rushed the few steps to her mother, engulfing her into her arms. They held one another for one long moment. "Oh, Mama, I waited so long for you to find me." Sobs left her as she cried, "Oh, Mama! Oh, Mama!"

"Yes, my Baby, we're together now. Don't ever forget it was Madame Marie who brung us together."

Letting go of Sissy and standing back to admire Sissy's maturity, Virginie's eyes spoke to Marie with gratitude. "Oh, madame! Oh, madame! You did bring my baby back to me."

"Yes, I did. And my baby? Is she asleep?"

"Yes, madame."

"Virginie, show Sissy where you both will sleep and wash her down and put a clean shift on her. Return her to me after she's washed, so we can talk."

Virginie took Sissy behind the cottage to the kitchen where she washed her in warm water and lavender soap and dressed her in a clean shift.

When Sissy returned to Marie in the dining room as Marie was having her tea, her sadness had left her, but she walked hesitantly, not sure of her role in this house. She waited until spoken to.

"Sissy, are you hungry?" Marie asked.

"No, madame."

"Would you like some tea?"

"No, madame."

"Would you like to see my baby?"

"Oh, yes, madame," Sissy answered with the first sign of delight in her voice. She followed Marie to her boudoir to find a rather large basket with a chair next to it.

They peered down into the basket. Still sleepy in the warmth of her blankets, Philomene opened her eyes to look up at her mother and Sissy.

"Oh, can I hold her?" Sissy's voice spiraled.

Marie heard joy in Sissy's voice and lifted the infant from her basket and placed her in the open arms of Sissy. "This is Philomene. Usually, she's crying to be fed, but she feels quite content in your arms. She likes you, Sissy."

"I love her. I want to take care of her. Can I take care of her, madame?"

"Yes, you will take care of Philomene and you must meet Marie Eucharist. She is sleeping now, but you will take care of her, too. Marie Eucharist is eight years old and studies with the Ursuline nuns. She will teach you everything she learns in school—your catechism, the history of this swampy place, and numbers. Then, you will be smart like her and will be able to go to market and haggle with the fish mongers and vendors."

Sissy's smile told Marie she was coming to life and feeling happy.

Chapter 33

In the tropical heat, every summer found an epidemic of yellow fever. Marie worked tirelessly to cure her people. Toward the end of summer, Marie found a need to rest as she was tired and pregnant with her fifth child.

At this time, Mama Antoine held voodoo services in her home.

A baby boy was born to Marie and Christophe. Sissy took delight in taking care of Archange Edouard. The Maraist children joined the Glapion children during their play times.

Archange died rather suddenly at the age of eight years. A state of depression took over Marie after losing her little boy.

One night after retiring to her boudoir, she breathed in the damp wind and the scent of the jasmines after a rainfall. Trying to relax her, Christophe joined her in their walnut bed and rubbed chamomile flower oil on her temples and kissed her passionately. In the cool darkness, he undressed her and massaged her breasts.

"Mon chere, I miss your love. Please do not turn away from me."

"I have not turned away from you my love. I mourn for our boy. He was the light of my life. Why did God take him away from me? Was it to punish me?"

"No, no, *mon chere*. He does not punish you nor would he ever have a reason to punish you. You only do good things for all of God's creatures. Archange is in heaven with the saints. He will watch over us. Please try to be happy for what we have. We have two beautiful daughters who adore you. Our Marie Eucharist watches everything you do and wants to be just like you."

"I will try to be happy." She held him tightly against her naked body while she let out solemn tears.

He stroked her back and kissed her thighs. "I want you to be the way you were, my love. The way you used to love me."

"I will try to love you the way that you want me to, my love." She tenderly kissed his hairy chest.

The tears that fell upon his bare chest tensed his muscles and aroused him before he made love to her. He thrusted hard inside of her until passion awakened inside of her trembling body. She moved in rhythm with his thrusts faster and faster until she felt they had become one, awash in the warm glow of his love. She screamed in her passion and then quieted. He continued thrusting, and she squeezed him inside of her body, still enjoying him, holding him tighter, feeling secure in his loving arms, until he gasped loudly and went limp.

Chapter 34

The summer of 1853 was particularly hot. People of means left town to go up north at the beginning of summer until the fall. Yellow fever had claimed more than one thousand citizens by the middle of July. New Orleanians had not been alerted so that a quarantine would not be placed on the city and trade would not suffer. The steamboats that brought trade to the city often carried passengers with their yellow fever and cholera upriver from New Orleans to other cities along the Mississippi River.

Eight-thousand people died that year out of 154,000 living in the city, marking the highest annual death rate of any state during the entire nineteenth century. The people did not realize that the mosquitoes breeding in their open wooden water cisterns were causing the yellow fever.

Marie worked tirelessly night and day to save her neighbors and friends. Those she grew up with who had yellow fever as a child and survived also had an immunity as Marie did and were able to nurse the fever patients without fear of catching the disease. The skill of the women of color in natural medicine was extraordinary. When an outsider would ask for their recipes, they refused, saying they would impart them only to their children.

Those most vulnerable to the diseases were newcomers to the area who were not acclimatized to the swampy, humid air and mosquitoes. Europeans were migrating to New Orleans in numbers and dying from the deadly disease.

Marie was called to a slave quarter flat where she found three children sprawled on a bed. As she looked down into their sweaty faces, their eyes were closed so that she could not tell how far they were gone. "Open your eyes," she told one boy. He lay limp, as she opened his eyelid to find yellowing eyes.

"Have they had any herbal tea at all?" Marie looked to the distraught mother.

"Yes, they had some this afternoon, but the nurse had to leave to see another family."

"Go to the house and ask madame for some ice. We must cool these children down."

"Yes, madame."

As the mother left the flat, Marie checked on the boys and removed their warm clothes. When the mother returned, she cried, "There is no ice, madame."

Marie took some cloths from her pocket. "Let's fan the boys with these cloths." She turned to the father on the floor. "Fan the boys while I go and try to find some cold water and brew some tea."

She walked across the courtyard and knocked on the back door of the main house. As a servant came to the door, Marie asked, "May I see your mistress? Tell her Marie Laveau wants to speak to her."

A white creole lady came to the door and looked into Marie's sad eyes.

"Madame, I am Marie Laveau, fever nurse. We desperately need ice for Nina's three boys. They are suffering from yellow fever and must be cooled down or they will die."

The lady put her hands over her face to hide her horror. "Oh, I'm so sorry. We have no ice."

"Have you tried to get some? Surely, you've seen the fever nurse go up to the slave quarter flat today."

"Yes, I've sent my servant to buy ice and they say with all the fever patients about the area, there is no more ice."

Marie tried to hide her dismay. "Can you bring us some cool water? I want to cool some rags to apply to the boys."

"Our water is hot from sitting in the hot cistern. I'm sorry to say that we have no cool water."

Marie reached into her pocket and pulled out herbal leaves. "Madame, may I go to your kitchen and brew herbal tea for Nina's boys?"

"Of course. I'll take you." The creole woman led Marie down the central hall of her home and out the back door to a building housing the kitchen. She instructed a servant to boil water for tea.

"The water must come to a boil first, and then these leaves must steep in the boiling water for ten minutes. Then, can you have your servant bring it up to the slave quarter, but tell her not to come inside lest she contract yellow fever. Just knock on the door, and I'll come to get it."

"I'll bring it up myself, madame, as soon as we steep the herbs. It's the least I can do. I've heard about you and how you've saved so many of my people. Thank you, madame." She bowed her head.

As Marie rushed out the door, she breathlessly uttered a thank you. "I'll go up and massage and fan the boys to cool them."

Saddened by the thought that she may not save Nina's boys, Marie walked across the courtyard and up the stairs to the slave quarter flat. As she entered, she heard sobs coming from Nina.

Nina was standing over one side of the bed, fanning her boys, while her husband was standing over the other side, fanning with tears in his eyes. "They're so still, madame. I don't know if they're alive!" she cried.

Marie hurried to feel one boy's hand, which felt like stone. She looked up at his mother, unable to speak.

Nina read the message in Marie's eyes. "He's gone. Isn't he?" She shrieked in pain as she fell to the floor. Marie went to her and held her. After a while, Marie tended to the other two boys, fanning them.

A knock on the door summoned Marie. As she took the teapot from madame's hands, she whispered, "One boy is gone."

The creole lady looked back with sadness as she walked away.

As Marie tried to get one brother to a sitting position to get him to drink, she saw that his body was lifeless and she wasn't able to get him to drink. She lay him back down and began to massage his arms and legs and his entire body to excite perspiration as his body felt cold, ready for death.

She went to his brother on the other side of the bed and found the boy in the same condition. She looked up to the father. "Rub like this on his arms and legs and body." The father did as Marie showed him, as she ran to the other side of the bed to resume massaging the brother.

Marie hated these times when she saw death at the door. She felt helpless with no cool water, no ice, and boys who were unable to lift their heads enough to drink her miraculous herbal tea that brought so many patients out of a fever and back to a fruitful life. When she saw no recovery in the boys, she knelt on the floor and began to pray. The mother and father knelt on the other side of the bed and joined Marie in her prayer. "Please, dear God, help us in our hour of need. Make us strong."

The parents kept repeating, "Make us strong, dear Lord. Make us strong," as they knelt beside their dying sons with no cool air, no cool water, but a killing fever that would snuff the life out of their children.

As all three of them realized that the boys were gone after feeling their bodies, they cried together.

⚜

Relieved to be out of the stifling, windowless room, smelling of sweat and vomit, Marie walked weakly in sadness toward her home on St. Ann, feeling guilty for the relief and for leaving three dead boys to their grieving parents. But she could not stay in that mournful room another minute, feeling that she could also fall sick.

As she made her way toward the river, she saw a little black girl, sitting in the dirt next to the road, holding her little brother, about one year old, in her arms. Marie bent her tired body low to look into the scared eyes of the little girl. "Where is your mama?"

The five-year-old girl pointed to the squealing wagon full of dead bodies being hauled away to the graves.

"Did they put your mama on one of those wagons?"

The girl nodded with dark frightening eyes.

"Is this your little brother?"

The girl nodded.

"You can come with me, and I'll take care of you." Marie put her hand out, but the girl looked up at her afraid to move. "I won't hurt you. I have two little girls you can play with. Are you hungry?"

The girl nodded once again.

"Come, child. I will carry your little brother. You can come to my home and eat." Marie reached out for the girl, and this time, she took Marie's hand.

They walked toward the cottage, and when they reached it, Marie felt exhausted and unable to take another step. "Virginie! Sissy!" she called out.

Unusual was the sound of Marie calling out so desperately, that Virginie heard urgency in her voice and ran to her with Sissy following.

"Virginie, these children have no mama. Take them and take care of them. I am feeling…"

"Yes, madame." Virginie took the young boy from Marie's arms, and Sissy took the girl's hand and led her away.

Christophe also appeared at the sound of his wife's plea for help. As he stepped toward her, she fell into his open arms. He carried her to their bed with worry. He had never seen her in such disarray.

"What is it, *mon chere*. Are you ill?"

"I have seen too much grief for one day, my love. And no sleep. I must rest. Please, look after the children. And see to the orphans I have brought home. They have no mama."

"Yes, yes, *chere*. Just rest." He covered his love with a duvet and watched her sleep.

Chapter 35

The biggest and most important celebration of the year among the racially mixed voodoo congregation was St. John's Eve, June twenty-third. Revelers had several means of public transit to Lake Pontchartrain where they celebrated on the shores. The Pontchartrain Railroad and the New Orleans and Spanish Fort Railroad transported all sorts and all colors to celebrate this festive time. Extra cars were added to the trains to accommodate the crowds for the spectacular occasion. Celebrants drove their buggies along the oyster-shell road along Bayou St. John. Coffee and gumbo stands set up along the river by the lakeside residents with bonfires illuminating them.

Many participants arrived in a lugger followed by a skiff carrying the voodoo queen, Marie Laveau, in full regalia, a green satin gown with matching tignon with seven points bearing every color of the rainbow and her gold, dangling earrings peeping down behind her black curls, caressing her light tan face. Fiery-lit candles swayed in the breeze behind her, as she stood on a platform, waving to the crowd. The magnificent sight of the voodoo queen hailed cheers and screams from the black and white congregation, who came for both spiritual cleansing and entertainment. Marie, who officiated when there was no fever epidemic, greeted with a creole song, Mamzelle Marie Chauffez, (Make it hot.) Drums rolled as each participant threw a piece of wood into a bonfire, making a wish. Marie said a prayer to the spirits as a cauldron was placed over the fire, and members walked past, throwing in salt, black pepper, a black snake cut into pieces, a black cat, a black rooster, and various powders. The contents was not eaten, but supposedly saved "for next year." Worshippers joined hands, sitting in front of the fires, as she preached a sermon. Then, they all knelt down to pray and receive her blessing.

People plunged into the lake where glowing fires could be seen along the shore as far as the eye could see. They sang, danced, ate gumbo and crawfish through the night.

At twilight, Marie encouraged people to leave. "Here is a new day. May the spirits guide you home to safety."

Chapter 36

Christophe was suffering from chest pains. Marie nursed him with indigenous herbs and a healthy diet from her garden. As the pains became more intense, he became weaker. Soon, he was unable to go to work to transact his real estate and slave trading business. Marie spent as much time as possible with him, encouraging him to rest.

As Marie sat at his bedside, Marie Eucharist entered. "Mama, a creole woman is here who looks most distressed. She asks to see you."

"I hate to leave papa. He may wake up and want me."

"I will sit with him, Mama. If he needs you, I will come and get you."

Marie looked apprehensive.

"Go, Mama. The woman needs you."

Marie left her boudoir and met the creole woman, sitting in her prayer room.

"Oh, I'm so glad to finally meet you, Madame Laveau. I am Madame Tremoulet."

Marie sat behind a small counseling table. "Madame, I'm here to help you. Tell me your problem."

"It is very difficult for me to talk about, madame, but I know from my friends that you are most discreet and able. My Harold has not been amorous with me lately. He used to have relations with me regularly and now, he does not come near me, not even for an embrace. When he leaves our home in the morning, he leaves no farewell, which is not like him."

"Does your husband leave in the evenings?"

"Yes. He just leaves and never says where he is going. I fear he has a lover."

"Madame, I have a concoction I have made myself. It is a perfume mixed with San Cipriano oil, which forces unfaithful mates to stop seeing other lovers. Just dab this perfume behind your ears and upon your wrists."

"Wonderful! I knew you would help me."

"Besides the perfume, there are other things you can do."

"And that is?" Madame Tremoulet's eyebrows went up in question.

"You can spread magnolia leaves beneath your mattress. It is said to make the most frigid couple passionate."

"*Oui,* madam, that sounds most delightful!"

"Another thing is that a new hairdo can do wonders to attract a husband."

"Oh, Madame, will you do my hair? I hear you are magnificent."

"I no longer do hair because my counseling and nursing keep me very busy, but my daughter, Marie Eucharist, has learned from me and is a very excellent hairdresser."

"I believe she is, if she learned from you, madame."

"Would you like her to come to your home in the morning?"

"Yes, I would love that. Here is my card with my address. I teach dancing in my home. If you know of anyone needing dance lessons, please refer them to me.

"Oui, madame, and may I ask you a personal question?"

"Madame Tremoulet hesitated for a moment. "Why, yes, madame."

Madame, do you go to Mass on Sundays?"

"Why, yes, I go every Sunday."

"Does your husband go with you?"

"No, not usually, unless it's a special occasion."

"Insist he go to Mass with you and pray that he prays, too. And insist he go to confession. Maybe he will see the light and realize he has a wife who loves him. Tell him that you love him every chance you get."

"I will follow your prudent advice, madame."

"Please wait for me while I get the perfume, madame." Marie returned with a small glass bottle and handed it to Madame Tremoulet.

"Thank you so much, madame. She placed two five dollar bills into Marie's hand.

"And thank you, madame. *Au revoir.*"

When Marie returned to her boudoir, she asked Marie Eucharist, "Has papa opened his eyes?"

"No, Mama, he is resting."

As Marie bent to look into her husband's face, she heard an owl hooting. *"Le Hibou,"* she said with fright in her widened, dark eyes. She believed the owl was threatening death. "Oh, Marie Eucharist, did you hear that?"

Marie Eucharist knew what her mother believed to be true.

"Go and get the priest, Marie."

The news had spread throughout the household that the priest was summoned to give papa his last rites.

Marie ran over all the things in her mind that she did for Christophe to make him well and couldn't think of what more to do for him. She felt his cold hand. "Oh, my dear husband, please don't leave me. I don't know what I'll do without you."

She knelt before the small altar in her boudoir and prayed for Christophe's recovery. "Please, Almighty God, make my loving husband well. I want him to live so that he may serve you. Please, God, help me to accept whatever is your will."

Marie Eucharist ushered the catholic priest in his black cassock, and purple stole hanging from his neck, into Marie's boudoir.

"Thank you for coming," Marie greeted with sadness, as she turned from her altar.

The priest walked immediately to Christophe and asked, "Would you like to enter into confession?" After receiving no response from the dying Christophe, he anointed his eyes, ears, nostrils, lips, hands, and feet with oil. He prayed, "May the Lord pardon thee whatever sins or faults thou hast committed." He turned to Marie. "I will pray for you to have strength in your time of sorrow. I will leave you now."

Feeling empty at the thought that she had no camaraderie with the priest as she had with Father Antoine, she felt anguish. Father Antoine would have embraced her and consoled her in her time of grief, but this priest did his duty and left as quickly as he came. *Oh, how I miss my friend, Father Antoine.*

She looked across at her husband with the mask of death. *And if I lose my dear husband, I will have no one.* Her heart ached with sadness. Then, she turned around to find her dear daughters, Marie Eucharist and Philomene, her grandchildren, her poor orphans that she sheltered, Virginie, and Sissy. They rushed to her and hugged her, each one showing their compassion and love. They knelt next to her and bowed their heads in prayer. Lawrence and Jude, her devoted slaves, stood humbly in the dark shadows of the boudoir and prayed for their master. Marie sat beside the walnut bed, waiting for Christophe to open his eyes, praying for one more glance from him to see his beautiful eyes.

Marie's family remained with her until Christophe took his last breath and passed away.

Chapter 37

Christophe had left many debts when he died, but Marie never let on that she had to work harder than ever to support her children, grandchildren, the orphans she had taken in, and her slaves.

In order to pay Christophe's debts, the cottage on St. Ann, that Marie was born and raised in, was auctioned off. Friends of the family rescued Marie by purchasing her home and generously allowing her and her family to live in it.

Privilege and prosperity for New Orleans free Creoles of color was soon coming to an end as the Black Codes were enforced.

In 1857, the law said that no slave shall be emancipated in this state. Slaves could no longer be freed by their masters or inherit their master's land.

The rich lives and privileged status of the free people of color vanished. They were banned from assembling or forming societies and were required to carry passes, observe curfews, and record racial status in all public records.

Free people of color, not born in Louisiana, would not be allowed entry by law. Police arrested free people of color daily charged with being against the law so much so that many attempted to pass themselves off as slaves. Free blacks were paying white men sums of money to testify that they had been born in Louisiana. Neighboring states did not allow people of African blood to remain in the state and be free and those that did not leave would be sold into slavery. Many free blacks went up north or to other countries and passed as white.

The president of Santo Domingo invited the free people of color to his country. Many went there and enjoyed equality of rights, which had been denied them in Louisiana. Many Louisianans said, "Good riddance. We can get along fine with our faithful slaves."

During this dangerous decade leading up to the Civil War, New Orleans lost its best writers, musicians, intellectuals, and leaders. Police raided many voodoo celebrations in private homes and on Lake Pontchartrain on the Eve of St. John's. In the bleakest hours, the black creole community turned to benevolent societies and to personal contact with the spirits, holding séances to contact the spirits of loved ones they had lost.

One sunny morning, Virginie was relating the turmoil going on in the neighborhood, as Marie ate her breakfast. "Monsieur Hogue got arrested last Saturday night coming home from confession."

Marie gave a ghastly look at Virginie and almost choked on her pain purdu. "That poor elderly man. I never heard of such blasphemy in my life."

"Coming home from church, he stopped in to visit a friend and lost track of the time. When he left his friend's home, the police arrested him and took him off to jail. And Monsieur Lebeuf got arrested yesterday for not having a paper on him that they asked for."

A female child ran through Marie's front door, running through the prayer room and into the dining room. "Madame, they took my papa to the jail. My mama is crying something awful. Can you help us?"

"Of course, Eulalie. Why did they take your papa to jail?"

"My mama has been crying that she misses the opera, so my papa went to buy opera tickets. The police arrested him and took him away. They said he had no right to go to the opera. My papa told me to run home and tell mama. I found mama at the French Market. Mama was buying papayas and the woman behind mama was yelling at the market lady selling the papayas and saying that her papayas were rotten. The market lady stuck her tongue out at the white lady. She did like this, madame." Eulalie stuck her tongue out as far as she could. "The market lady didn't say anything to the white lady. She just did this." Eulalie demonstrated, once again, her tongue sticking out as far as she could. "Then, the policeman, as fast as a cat, ran up to the market lady and arrested her and took her off to jail."

"I will go directly to the police and straighten this out." Marie got up from the table to get her shawl. When she returned, she saw the child eyeing her pain perdu. "Have you had breakfast, Eulalie?"

The child lowered her head and moved it back and forth.

"Virginie, feed the child some pain perdu." She turned to the young girl. "Eat your breakfast now, and then go home and tell your mama that your papa will be home soon."

When Marie arrived at the police station, she asked for the new Chief of Police, as Monsieur Hebert had retired as Chief of Police. "Tell him Marie Laveau wishes to speak to him."

When the Chief of Police entered the waiting room, Marie rose, and said, "I am Marie Laveau."

"And what brings you here, Marie Laveau?"

"I understand your police arrested a senior citizen who lives in our community, a Monsieur Hogue. He was coming from church and stopped in to see a friend. And also a Monsieur Trosclaire was arrested for purchasing opera tickets."

"Yes. I read the records. Monsieur Hogue violated his curfew."

"It was but a few moments after the curfew," she said, "because the elderly man walks very slowly."

"Nevertheless, he violated the curfew. And Monsieur Trosclaire dared to join the free people at the opera. Such insolence to think he can live as white people," he retorted flippantly.

Annoyed by his remark, Marie looked him in the eye with a scornful look. "You differentiate between people of color and white people. They are not to congregate together, but who do you call when your child has the fever?" She paused and stepped back with a stare. "Now, I remember you."

"And I know of you," he said.

"Who did you call when your son was in the third day of yellow fever? You didn't call a white doctor, did you? You called on me, begging me to come and save your son from dying. You offered a seat in your coach to sit next to you. Otherwise, I cannot sit next to a white person.

And I came to you, a woman of color, to save your white son. I didn't discriminate when I saw he was a white boy. I saved him from dying, and now you tell me you have a man of color, born in Louisiana, locked up in a jail cell for wanting to take his wife to the opera? Tell me what you will do when your daughters or your wife gets the fever? The fever season will start soon."

"I thank you, madam, for saving my son."

"Answer me. Who will you call when your daughters or your wife gets the fever?"

"I, uh, would most humbly call upon you, madame. Your reputation supersedes you."

"I don't think you should bother, monsieur. I am a person of color, don't forget, and I should not congregate with you or enter a white person's home. And perhaps, if these arrests continue, I will decide to move out of the city, and the black fever nurses will follow me. And where will you be when your head sizzles in a fever and your eye balls are yellow?"

"I respectfully will release Monsieur Hogue, as he is an old man who walked slowly and also Monsieur Trosclaire."

"And I will follow you as you release them."

As Marie followed the Chief of Police down the hall to the jail cells, five men of color on the other side called out to her. "Please, Madame Laveau, get me out of jail." They banged on the bars to get her attention.

The Chief of Police unlocked the cells of Monsieur Hogue and Monsieur Trosclaire.

"Thank you, madame." Monsieur Hogue's eyes misted with appreciation.

"I most humbly thank you, madame," Monsieur Trosclaire said.

Marie turned to face the jailed men on the other side. "And these! They must all be released."

The Chief of Police faced her, indignant, ready to refuse her request. Then, as he hesitated, he thought of his son lying in fever and Marie cooling him, icing him for hours, and feeding him her herbs. He stood silent for a long moment, as she squinted toward him, lifting her chin, and challenging him.

He walked slowly to the other side and unlocked the first cell. The jailed man took her hand and kissed it. "My children are waiting for me, madame. My wife has died, and I am all they have. God bless you."

The man of color's story encouraged the Chief of Police to open the next cell. He hesitated in silence, but then the banging on the bars with their metal cups encouraged him to open the next three cell doors. The men congregated in the small hall between the cells and thanked Marie.

"Before we leave, we shall collect all of your belongings," Marie said.

The Chief of Police gave her a look of surprise. "But...

"Surely, you've confiscated their gold watches and wallets, and they must be returned. Follow me, gentlemen."

Marie walked without hesitation, walking in her straight, proud walk with her head held high, the men following her to a front office.

The Chief of Police followed lastly in awe, never quite knowing a woman in such command.

As they walked to another room to be checked out and retrieve their belongings, they passed a small room with two cells on each side. A woman screamed out to Marie. "Widow Paris, please get me out of here!"

Marie stopped to look inside the small jail cell room. "Let's proceed ahead," the Chief of Police said.

Ignoring his remark, Marie entered the small room to find the locked woman. "Please, madame, get me out of here."

"Are you the woman who works at the French Market?"

"Yes, madame."

"Do you sell papayas and mangoes?"

"Yes, madame. I will lose my business if I don't get back to my stand."

"I'll get you out. I must talk to the Chief of Police."

As the men were signing out of jail and retrieving their wallets and gold watches, Marie called out to the Chief of Police. "Monsieur, that lady in the jail cell. Why is she jailed?"

"She was accused of insulting a white woman."

"I happen to know she didn't say one word to that white lady."

"How would you know that? Were you there?"

"My neighbor was there and my neighbor does not lie. She was there when the market lady was arrested."

"Madame, you see, this is a special case. She insulted a very prominent lady in the city, and it went to court. She can not be released without full bail."

"In other words, this is your way of keeping her in jail. How much is the bail?"

"Three-hundred and fifty dollars."

The released men were waiting for Marie. Some of them were waiting for their belongings. "Gentlemen, they have arrested a woman they have locked up in that small room. I happen to know she did not insult the woman who accuses her. Her bail is set at three hundred and fifty dollars. Between all of you, can we raise the bail money?" Marie asked.

"I'm sure that between us, we can raise the money," Monsieur Hogue said.

"Of course, madame," Monsieur Trosclaire said. The other men agreed.

"Now, check your wallets and make sure your cash is there and the passes you must carry with you.

We don't want this charade to happen again," Marie said.

"Monsieur Hogue, is your pass in your wallet?" Marie asked.

The old man went through his wallet and nodded.

"Did you get your watch returned?"

"Yes, I believe so," the man replied.

"Gentlemen, check your cash and papers. Make sure they are all there," Marie warned.

After a moment, the men left the police station. Marie followed and found them outside, waiting for her. "Madame, we've agreed to put our money together for the bail. We must first go to the bank to secure cash. Will you accompany us to the bank, and then we can proceed back to the police station?" Monsieur Trosclaire asked.

"Yes, that would be fine," Marie said.

Monsieur Trosclaire opened the door to a coach and tipped his hat. "After you, madame. Monsieur Hogue and Monsieur Trosclaire joined Marie for the ride to the bank. The five other men followed in another coach.

At the bank, the seven men of color gave Marie fifty dollars each so that Marie could bail the Market Lady out of jail.

The men chauffeured Marie home and the Market Lady to her fruit stand before her papayas and mangoes could spoil.

Chapter 38

The Civil War broke out in 1861. Slaves and free blacks joined the army, many becoming black officers under a white colonel. If a white plantation owner owned twenty-five or more slaves, he was not required to fight. When the black soldiers realized they were fighting for the white plantation owners to keep their slaves, they went to fight with the north. The Union Soldiers occupied New Orleans in 1862, the first southern city to be occupied during the Civil War and remained so during the duration of the war.

Marie always stayed faithful to the south and helped the confederate soldiers by bandaging their wounds and giving them shelter, as she and her mother did in the Battle of New Orleans in 1815.

One morning, as Marie left her home to buy indigenous herbs from the Choctaw Indian women, she saw a confederate soldier lying in the road. She went to find him in a weak, wounded state, bleeding from his chest.

"Can you get up?" she asked.

"I don't know," he answered.

She could tell by his voice he was a young boy who reminded her of her son, Archange, who might have been this soldier if he had lived. "Let me take you to my home," she said.

"I don't know if I can…"

"Come, I'll help you," she urged, as she helped him up. She struggled to get him to her cottage.

As she got him through her front door, she called for her slave. "Lawrence, come and help us!"

As the slave appeared, he took hold of the young soldier, relieving Marie. "Where shall I take him, madame?"

"Take him to the outbuilding where you sleep. I want to hide him until he is well."

The burly slave carried the young soldier through the cottage and out back to the small building where he slept and laid him on his cot.

Marie ran for her bag under the dining room table and followed them to the outbuilding. "Help me take his jacket off," Marie instructed. As they stripped off his jacket, the blood pooled on his chest. She waded through the blood with her fingers and unbuttoned his shirt. Grabbing a towel from her bag with bloody hands, she placed it on his chest wound, and applied direct pressure to the wound for a full five minutes.

The young soldier moaned and thrashed from side to side in pain as Marie steadied the towel over the wound and soaked up the blood. She threw the blood-soaked towel on the floor and applied another towel to the wound. "You're almost over the worst part. You'll be fine. Just bear with me. I'll take care of you. Open your eyes," she asked the soldier.

He looked down at her and then closed his eyes, trusting her soothing voice and her promise to clean his wound.

"You feel hot," she said, as she felt his forehead with her forearm.

"Yes, I'm hot," he said.

He opened his eyes again, as she peered into them and felt relieved that she saw no yellow tinge in his eyes that she thought beautiful, because they were the blue color of her son's, Archange, and his skin had the same bronzy tone. *Thank you, God.* She surmised he did not have yellow fever but did have a temperature. "What is your name?" she asked, as she searched for the bullet.

"Quentin," he said.

"Quentin, nice." She nodded.

As she spotted the bullet, she reached into her bag for bullet forceps and pulled the bullet from his flesh.

The boy let out a moan and scrunched his face in pain.

She cleaned his wound with compact cotton bandages and applied her herbal ointment to bandages she covered the wound with.

"You will feel better now. Just rest. You're safe here. The Union Soldiers won't find you, but if they should come here, I will tell them you're my slave, and that you can't speak. Can you pretend you can't speak if a Union soldier finds you?"

The boy nodded, and a gentle smile left his face.

"And you, Lawrence, I will say you're crippled and can't walk. If a soldier comes here, either side, just stay on the floor. I don't want them taking you off. I need you here. One more thing. We have to get rid of the uniform." She turned to Lawrence. "Help me get his trousers off. I want you to burn them along with his shirt and jacket out back behind the cookhouse. Also, ask Virginie for a black cloth sack and put his boots in the sack and bury the sack out back."

They tugged the trousers off the boy. "Now, go and come back here after you've burned the uniform and buried the boots."

"Yes, Boss Lady." Lawrence hurried out the door.

She looked down at the boy, wiping his forehead, and stayed with him in the musty room until Lawrence returned.

When Lawrence returned, she asked. "Did you burn the uniform and bury the boots?"

"Yes, Boss Lady."

"Good. You stay with him. Don't leave his side. I will go and buy him some civilian clothes. Virginie will come with water for him. Offer him water and let him drink. I will be back as soon as I can."

Her arms were filled with clothes for the young boy. "Help me put a shirt on him," she told Lawrence. "We have to hide his wound in case they come here."

They put a shirt on Quentin, as the boy grimaced when they moved his arms.

"He is perspiring. I must get some herbal tea. Here, wipe his face and neck," she said, as she handed Lawrence the cloth from her bag.

She returned with a kettle of herbal tea and put the cup of tea to his lips. He took small sips as she patiently fed him.

"Please, God, let this stop his fever," she whispered.

"I can give it to him," Lawrence obliged.

"No, you rest on the floor. I may need you later when I am too tired to stay awake."

Lawrence retired to the floor, as Marie nursed Quentin, changing his bandages throughout the night to keep the wound clean and opened the door to let the cool evening breeze cool the room. Quentin fell asleep, writhing in pain. Lawrence snored wildly while Marie stayed awake and prayed so that Quentin would not fall into a deeper fever from his infected wound.

Marie dozed off for a short time. The sound of footsteps approaching woke her. She prayed it was not a Union Soldier.

Virginie appeared in the doorway to the relief of Marie. "Madame, I could barely sleep, worrying about the young man. I brought some cool rain water to quench his thirst."

"Thank you, Virginie. I'll offer it to him as soon as he wakes up." She walked to Quentin to feel his forehead. "He's still in a fever. I have to get some ice to cool him. Can you stay with him while I buy some ice? And I'll have to buy some more herbs for his pain."

"Of course, madame."

"If he wakes, offer him some water."

Returning with ice filled rags, Marie applied them to Quentin's head and chest to reduce inflammation. She fed him herbal tea to relieve his pain. After several days, the fever subsided.

As Marie was spoon-feeding Quentin soup, Sissie ran into the slave quarter room. "Madame, a Union Soldier is in the main house. He's asking if we're hiding any soldiers. He's in the upstairs room in the main house, snooping under the beds."

"Where is Lawrence?" Marie asked in an urgent voice.

"He's in the cookhouse."

"Run there and tell him to come here right away. He must sit on the floor like I told him before the Union Soldier comes snooping here. He must run here fast."

Sissy ran out of the room with speed. Lawrence appeared with fright in his eyes.

"Get down on the floor, and remember what I told you. You are a crippled person who can't walk." Marie covered Lawrence with a blanket and looked over at Quentin. "And remember, you can't talk!"

Marie sat next to the cot and resumed feeding Quentin soup from a spoon when the Union Soldier barged in, stomping his heavy leather boots, one by one, on the roughly hewn wooden floor to announce himself.

"And who do we have here?" he roared with a wide grin.

"My two disabled slaves," Marie answered.

"Disabled? In what way?"

"My young slave here can't talk."

"And what about him?" He pointed to Lawrence, lying on the floor.

"He is quite crippled. He can't walk."

"Hmphh. Is that so? Seems to me I've heard that story before. Can't he work?" He pointed to Quentin.

"Oh, no! He is suffering from yellow fever. He is hot. See the yellow in his eyes?"

The Union Soldier grimaced and backed up so fast, he nearly fell over. His face fell into scorn, squinting at Marie and puffing up his nose. "Why didn't you tell me that in the first place?"

"You ran in here so fast, I didn't get a chance."

"Well, aren't you afraid you'll catch that horrible yellow jack, too?"

"I never know. I can have it as we speak."

"Yee gads, woman," he croaked, as he hightailed out the door. Marie smiled and looked down at Lawrence, covering his mouth with his large hands, muffling a laugh. She was happy to see Quentin smiling in a broad grin for the first time. She held her finger to her lips, shaking her head, warning them not to laugh out loud in case the Union Soldier was within earshot.

They kept quiet and then heard rustling outside. *Is he coming back? Is another Union Soldier snooping around outside?*

Their expressions changed from relief to freight. They remained silent as they heard more footsteps outside. As the door pushed open, Sissy entered breathing heavily.

Her eyes widened as she announced, "He's gone, madame. Yeh, he ran outta here pretty fast, never stopped for nothin'."

Lawrence was the first to let out a big roar of laughter, and Quentin laughed at him. Marie was so happy to see Quentin laugh, she let out a big belly laugh.

Sissy looked down at Lawrence, then at Quentin, and then at Marie. She scratched her head. "What's everybody laughin' about?"

Chapter 39

In the days that followed, Union Soldiers were taking over plantations and pillaging from homes. Many invaded homes, looking for Confederate Soldiers. The Union Soldiers paced the streets making many women nervous, but some women lifted their skirts, exposing their shapely legs and bottoms out of defiance. Many women were known to have dumped their chamber pots on them from their balconies and spit on their heads.

The occupation leaders stated a decree, "Woman Order," stating that any woman who insulted a United States Army Officer would be considered a prostitute.

Many families without fathers went hungry. Marie took vegetables and fruits from her garden to feed them.

In spite of the devastation and the horrors of the war with men returning without arms and legs, Marie's home was a relatively happy place with her grandchildren living with her and her canaries chirping in their cages.

She brought Quentin back to health but refused to let him go back to the war. She feared the Union Soldiers would kill him or put him in a Prisoner of War Camp, where many soldiers died of infectious diseases from unsanitary conditions and bad food, so she kept him within the confines of her home. Quentin began to enjoy Marie's motherly care and working with Lawrence in the garden. Lawrence planted more vegetables than ever so that they could share with those that didn't have enough to eat.

Marie was praying at her altar in her prayer room, when she heard a loud bang on her door. Upon opening it, a Confederate Soldier stood tall in front of her, his medals on his uniform gleaming back at her.

"Madame, Captain Duplantier here. I was told you may be able to help me."

"Do come in."

He entered rather hastily and gave a loud sigh.

"However did you get past them?" she asked, placing her hands on the side of her face.

"It wasn't easy. I hid in a coach and paid dearly to get here. I have a terrible cold, madame, and it has lingered for a long time. Can you give me something for it?"

"Please, sit down." She noticed his harried look. "Rest yourself and I'll brew some herbal tea for you."

The officer sat and when Marie returned, she handed him a cup of warm, herbal tea. As he reached for the cup, he fell to the floor. She knelt to feel his pulse, which assured her that he was alive. She went to the dining room and opened the door to the yard and called for Lawrence.

Lawrence was attuned to Marie's voice and hurried to the house. "Lawrence, I need you to carry a soldier to my boudoir."

"Yes, madame."

Upon noticing his muddy boots, Marie said, "Let's pull his boots off. I don't need this mud in my boudoir." Lawrence pulled the officer's boots off and carried him to Marie's boudoir.

"On my bed, Lawrence. The man is exhausted from this hellish war." She placed her finger to her lips. "Don't tell anyone he is here. The Union Soldiers may be looking for him. They could kill him. Remember. Don't tell."

"Yes, madame." Lawrence nodded.

She ran through her house and out the front door to see if the coach was waiting. "Please, leave. The soldier is in need of medical care. And please keep this secret or they will kill him."

She watched the coach leave and returned to her boudoir to find the soldier lying on her bed. He turned his head toward her, as he heard her come in. "I am so sorry, madame. I don't know what happened. One minute, I'm sitting in a chair and the next thing I know, I'm on a fine bed."

"No need to apologize. In this time of war, stranger things have happened."

"What did just happen?"

"You passed out. You are so congested and fully exhausted. Here, drink this." She handed him a cup of herbal tea.

He graciously took it and drank. Looking down, he asked, "Where are my boots?"

"Don't worry. Lawrence is cleaning them. We'll return them to you."

"Of course," he said. "My head pounds."

"You should rest. I'll return later with more herbs."

"I didn't intend to put you out like this, madame."

"You are a soldier, and I am a Creole. We're both fighting in this war, maybe not for the same thing, but we're fighting together. Just rest. Do not fret about putting me out."

Captain Duplantier had more than a cold. He had a case of influenza and complete exhaustion. He stayed until Marie restored him to health. He became acquainted with Quentin who he had much in common with. They were both from northern Louisiana.

Marie checked him one morning to find he had no fever. "Your fever is gone, and I'd say you're on your way to good health. Will you join Quentin, my daughter, Philomene, and me in the dining room for breakfast?"

"I'd be delighted to, madame."

He stepped into the dining room with baggy cotton pants and shirt that Marie had secured for him. "*Bonjour,*" he greeted with a broad smile.

Marie looked up to him, thinking he looked quite well. "*Bonjour*, Captain."

He peered out of the open door. "Who are the lovely children, playing in the yard?" he asked.

"They are my grandchildren, Philomene's children, Alexandre, four, Fidelia, three, and Noemie, just one year old. They've been running in and out of your room all week, wanting to see you."

"Beautiful children from a beautiful mother." He bowed to Philomene. "I most sincerely apologize to you. I've been so delirious in a fever that I've hardly noticed who was coming in and who was bringing in my medicinal herbs and food. Please forgive me for my absentmindedness," the captain said, as he looked at Philomene and then at Marie.

Philomene's flowering face looked up to the captain. "No need to apologize, captain. Thank you for your service to our country."

"I am much obliged to you and your mother for saving my life," the captain said.

Quentin, dressed in slave's clothes so as not to draw attention to him, looked up to the captain with admiration. *"Bonjour."*

The captain nodded.

"I'm sorry it's so meager—just eggs and Virginie's home made bread," Marie said apologetically.

"The aroma is spellbinding. I can't wait to eat it," the captain said.

Quentin shoved the warm bread in his mouth without a word.

Virginie came in with fresh orange juice and poured it in their glasses. "God bless our orange trees," Virginie said.

"Yes, they're a blessing, aren't they?" Marie said.

"Most certainly," the captain agreed, as he gulped down the juice.

"I'll bring in hot coffee as soon as it's brewed," Virginie said.

Marie, wanting to hear some war news, looked across the table at the captain. "Now that your head is clear, tell me a little about how the war was going up north of here."

"Well, the northern states were short of soldiers a while back. Then, President Lincoln emancipated the slaves, and they all went to fight with the north, about a hundred thousand of them. Ever since, the south has been short of soldiers. The Union has three times as many soldiers as we have in the south."

"It's madness—this war. I want it to end," Marie said. "The creole people don't even care who wins. We just want it to end."

Virginie came in with the steaming coffee pot and poured for everyone.

"Lee surrendered! Lee surrendered!" They heard screaming in the street. Everyone ran out front to see boys, girls, men, and women running through the streets wild with excitement.

Marie looked inquisitively at a woman running by. "The war is over! Lee surrendered!" More crippled men passed the house, some with bells, some with horns, some walking with canes. The cathedral bells clanged without stop.

"You can go home now, Quentin. You're free from the army," Marie said.

Quentin hugged Marie. "This is the happiest day of my life. Thank you for saving me, madame. I wouldn't be here if not for you."

"Alleluia," shouted Virginie. "I gotta go tell Lawrence what all the fuss is about."

"Thank God for the end of the mayhem," the captain said.

Marie's neighbor, Diehlia, walked over and embraced Marie with tears in her eyes.

Marie went home and knelt in her prayer room and thanked God for peace. The others followed and prayed with her.

As Virginie was leaving the cookhouse, she saw Lawrence digging a big hole. "What're you planting there?" she asked.

"I'm not a plantin'. I'm a diggin'."

"What're you a diggin'?"

She saw him reach into the hole and pull out a large, black, cloth bag.

With a broad grin, he lifted the black bag above his head. "I found it. I was pretty sure I buried it here almost two years ago. He unfolded the bag and pulled out a pair of army boots."

"You don't say!" Virginie looked as happy as Lawrence.

"Yep. They're Quentin's army boots. I got some black polish. I'm goin' ta spiffy them up for him. He'll be so happy."

Quentin came up as Lawrence was cleaning the army boots on the grass. "Do you recognize these?" Lawrence asked.

"Are those my...?" He stared at his boots and let out a bark of laughter. "I've been barefooted for so long, I wonder if I could get boots back on my feet."

"Oh, you'll get 'em on. Madame, got you a pair of socks to go with your boots. They'll go over the socks."

Quentin watched Lawrence clean and shine his boots in anticipation of trying them on. "Okay, now, let's go in and you put on a nice pair of pants and a nice shirt to go with your shiny boots. We don't want your mama to think we didn't take good care of you."

They went in the outbuilding where they slept, and Quentin found a clean pair of pants and a shirt lying on his cot. "Here, put these on," Lawrence urged.

"Where'd they come from?" Quentin asked.

"Madame put them there for you. She said she wanted your mama to see you lookin' good."

Quentin quickly dressed and sat on his cot to put on his new socks. Lawrence sat on the floor and helped Quentin on with his boots. "Okay, now step down hard," Lawrence urged. Quentin stepped down hard on the rough wooden floor several times until he felt his feet fit his boots.

"Thanks so much, Lawrence. You've been swell. Just like a brother."

Lawrence embraced Quentin. "I'm gonna miss you, brother. Who's gonna help me with the plantin'?"

"I'll come back and stay with you again."

"I sure hope that happens."

Captain Duplantier, preparing to leave Marie's home, left cash on Marie's bedside table.

Marie stood in the doorway of her boudoir to see him peering in the looking glass in full uniform, smoothing down his hair before he put his hat on, his medals gleaming, his crimson worsted waist-sash wrapped around his waist, looking strikingly handsome. She looked across the room at him and thought she never realized he was as handsome as he was. He reminded her of the first time she saw Christophe dressed in full uniform.

She hated to break the silence and wanted to stand there for a moment to admire him, but he turned to her and smiled. "*Bonjour*," she said.

"*Bonjour*." He joined her, and they walked through the house out the front door into the cool air.

"Thank you ever so much, madame, for saving my life and offering your home as a lovely, safe haven. How can I ever repay you?"

"Can you see that Quentin gets home safely? I'm sure that his mother is worried sick about him, not knowing if he's dead or alive."

"You can rest assured, madame, that I will see to it that Quentin gets home safely. I will personally take him to his door."

Marie didn't understand the swelling feeling she felt in her heart for a man she knew only for a couple of weeks. She looked at him with feeling, and he seemed to understand the feeling that he also felt.

He embraced her. "I hate to leave you. May I come to see you again when I am in New Orleans?"

"Yes, you may."

The mood was broken when Quentin ran outside in his shiny boots, looking happy to go home. The captain stepped back, and Quentin took his place in a warm embrace with Marie. "I can't thank you enough, madame, for saving me and taking such good care of me. Just like I was your son. Thank you."

"You are like my son, Quentin. Come back to see me when you can. I would like that very much."

"I will, madame."

The captain hailed a coach that was approaching. It stopped. Quentin threw Marie a kiss and jumped into the coach. The captain stood with one hand on the door handle and stood with a sad look at Marie. He bowed to Marie and boarded the coach. He looked at her through the window as if to say *I want to stay with you. I want to see if we have something for each other.* He kissed his fingers and waved to her.

She waved back and ran into the house with a pounding heart so that he wouldn't see her tears.

Chapter 40

1881...In the twilight of her life when her grandchildren were grown, Marie no longer worked long hours except for the occasional consultation.

On Sunday afternoons after mass, Marie would walk to where Congo Square once was, where slaves and free people of color danced. Slowly but still straight in her blue cotton dress, her tignon in bright multi-colors, creatively wrapped in nine points, perched on her head, golden earrings dangling, she looked ahead to where merry serenaders used to sing and greet passers-by under balconies. As she approached one familiar balcony, she heard the sweet voices serenading her and sang along with them to herself, her heart feeling every beat of the song. When she passed this balcony, she looked back and no one stood there. She looked up to see if the singing came from above. A toddler stood on the balcony above, grasping the bars with his tiny hands, staring down at Marie with sad eyes. Marie looked up to him, smiled, and prayed that his mother would soon come to him and take his sadness away and make him smile.

She walked across Rue Rampart to a bench facing the area where Congo Square once was with live oaks nestled in rows before her. In her mind's eye, she saw male and female slaves forming a ring and one at a time danced in rhythmic movements and gesticulations with great agility to the beat of African tom-toms. The men, covered only with a sash around their bodies, otherwise naked except for the little bells and shells flirting about their arms and legs, stood straight. They appeared to puff out their chests as they waited for their ladies to join them. The women modestly wore dresses, trying to imitate the latest fashions of the day as best they could.

Banjos strummed among drums, rattles, and jawbones. And amid the music, she remembered how the men would bow and the ladies would curtsy. A male Bamboula dancer would step into the ring and start his dance and chants. "Aye ya yi." He'd dance over to the lady and take her hand, guiding her into the circle, stand her before him and dance the Bamboula for her. During the fervor of the frantic music, another couple would enter the ring and start their Bamboula ritual, and then another couple would enter. The dancers danced until they dropped and were pulled out of the ring.

She heard the clapping hands of the spectators and the cheers, screaming for more. She saw her friends, long gone, cheering them on, and they watched the Bamboula in a great frenzy. She heard the drum rhythms, pulsing like the blood in her veins.

She hummed the songs the black slave women would sing that the white creole women did not recognize themselves in. The white creole women had not paid attention to women of color in the same room, even in their boudoirs, and had not realized the black women understood their French and learned their intimate secrets.

Marie smiled to herself as she thought of the many secrets she learned in the white women's boudoirs as she dressed their hair. How could they not recognize themselves in these songs? The verses came to mind.

> I am a creole maid,
> More beautiful than my mistress.
> I have stolen pretty things from
> Madame's Armoire
> Danse Colinda, Danse Colinda
> Boudoum, Boudoum
>
> I have taken a few silk scarves
> That made my mistress look sallow
> And I borrowed madame's husband as well
> Danse Colinda, Danse Colinda
> Boudoum, Boudoum

In her reverie, she stood and clapped and was about to cheer the dancers on to dance more exotically and more sensually, as the drums beat faster and faster, when she closed her eyes and saw the dancers slow and drop in exhaustion.

In her mind, the dancers grew tired, as she felt tired. But then she thought of the day she met Jacques in this very spot as he followed her as she was leaving and asked if he could buy her a drink. She had gone with him for a drink, and he walked her home, and she knew that very day that he had something for her. *He was such a handsome, hardworking man. Why did he leave me? Did he not believe that I loved him? I loved that man so much.*

She still pictured General Jackson on the day he entered the square that bears his name in January 1815 when they celebrated the victory of the Battle of New Orleans.

And then she recalled the joy at the end of the Civil War with people cheering in the streets, tooting horns and ringing tiny bells and cathedral bells clanging away continuously. And a week later, we lamented the death of our dear President Lincoln. The church bells tolled for peace and happiness at the end of the war, and then the bells tolled again for sadness and mourning. That great president freed the people of color, but men made laws not to make them equal. Everybody, small or great, rich or poor lamented the death of that great man, who freed the slaves.

As she rested in the afternoon tropical heat, listening to the Colinda songs that made her smile, friends came by whom she had served during her lifetime and brought her fruit syrups over ice. Many were drawn to her as they remembered what sacrifice or kindness she had shown them. Always someone would sit with her and keep her company. Marie never sat alone for very long.

She felt she wanted coffee, and walked to Rose Nicaud's coffee stand. *"Café au lait, s'il vou plait."* She reached into her pocket for piasters.

"No, no, no, madame. Gratis. We will bring your coffee to you. Please sit and rest."

Tables and chairs stood outside for relaxation. People brought their coffee to the tables, but Marie was served by a young woman. *"Café au lait*, madame. And *lagniappe.* Madame Nicaud said to take you a slice of her sweet potato bread."

"Merci." Marie said with a smile, and turned to smile in Madame Nicaud's direction.

Sometimes, she didn't know the people who joined her, but they knew her.

Philomene was looking for her mother and found her having coffee amid friends. "Oh, there you are, Mama. I should have known."

"It is lovely to have coffee outside on such a beautiful day among friends," Marie replied.

"Yes, Mama. I know you are enjoying yourself, but you must be tired by now."

"When I am having a good time, I forget I am tired."

Philomene waited until Marie finished her coffee and took her mother home.

In her last year, Marie spent much of her time resting either in bed or on her yard in the sunshine. Philomene took care of her mother as did Virginie, who stayed with her after the emancipation of the slaves. Lawrence also stayed on as he couldn't find a job. The good jobs were taken by the white men, which left only hard labor jobs for the men of color. Jude, Marie's other slave, never returned from the Civil War. Sissy married and moved away.

Doting on her mother one morning, Philomene said, "Mama, why don't you just take it easy, and I'll bring your breakfast to your bed."

"Oh, you're always fussing over me, Daughter. Why doesn't Marie Eucharist ever bring me my tea or my breakfast?"

"Mama, Marie Eucharist is gone."

"Gone? Gone where?"

"She passed a while ago, Mama."

"I don't remember that."

"It was so terrible for you that you put it out of your mind."

"*Mon Dieu.* Did I pray for her?"

"Yes, Mama, you prayed for her."

"It's funny how I remember so many things that have happened in my life, but I don't remember that."

Philomene propped Marie's pillows up to make a comforting spot for her back and distract her. "After breakfast, Mama, we'll go out on the yard, and I'll pick some fruit for you."

As Marie sat on her yard on a cushioned chaise longue in front of a trellis laced with summer vines and listened to her canaries chirping, Philomene came to her. "Mama, a reporter from The Picayune is here to speak to you. Do you feel up to talking to him and answering questions?"

"Yes, I can speak and answer questions. Bring him out."

The reporter came outside and greeted in the manner white Americans had adopted for addressing black women. "*Bonjour*, Mama Marie. Francois Curet at your service."

"*Bonjour*, Monsieur Curet."

"I want to ask you about voodoo," he said. "My colleagues on The Picayune have called it fetish devil worship of heathen Africa and that the dances at the lakefront are bestial performances with the wildest and most hellish orgies."

"Ah! And you, young man, do you believe everything you hear or do you seek the facts?"

"I seek the facts."

"Well, then you have come to the right place. I am no voudou now. I am a believer in the holy faith. I am a member of the Roman Catholic Church where I was baptized and married two times. Many of the articles written about me in the newspapers were taken from gossip. They wrote that I practiced witchcraft and had a large snake that I wrapped around my neck. They wrote that I had fifteen children. None of that was true."

"None of it?"

"None of what I just mentioned. I was not a witch. I told people what they wanted to believe. I never had a large snake that I wrapped around my neck for God's sake. I had seven children with my late husband, Christophe Glapion, and one before that who died as an infant. Three of my children were born dead that I never even got to hold. I have had nine grandchildren who lived with me, off and on, and three still do. I took in orphans from the streets who lived with me. Only one of my seven children still lives, and she is right here, my beautiful Philomene."

"I can see why reporters thought you had fifteen children."

"You can? Then, you are as lazy and dim witted as the reporters who did not report the truth. Why didn't they get the facts? You rash writers with your great imaginations only report what you imagine, not what is real."

"I must apologize for the reporters, Mama Marie."

"Tell them that voodoo has changed and adapted much faster than they have and your newspaper, The Picayune."

"Does voodoo still exist?" he asked.

"Yes, it still exists."

Philomene rose and walked to her mother. "I see that my mother's eyes are tiring. I must take her in to rest. Will you please excuse us, monsieur?"

"Of course. *Au revoir.*"

He bowed as Marie saw his eyes follow her as Philomene helped her to the cottage with the aid of her cane.

Marie awakened by a hooting owl outside her boudoir. She called for Philomene.

As Philomene came to her bedside, Marie widened her coal black eyes. *"Le Hibou.* I think it's time for you to call the priest, *chere.* The owl sees death."

Philomene had dreaded this moment and ran for the priest. She returned with the priest dressed in a black suit with white, Roman collar and purple stole hanging from his neck. When they entered Marie's boudoir, Marie said, *"Chere,* will you please leave us so that Father can hear my last confession?"

"Yes, Mama."

The priest walked over to Marie who held a small crucifix. "Madame Laveau, God will welcome you, a most dedicated person to His work, and you will live in eternal peace." He then blessed Marie with holy water.

Marie wasted no time to begin her confession. "Bless me, Father, for I have sinned. My last confession was a week ago. I have lied, Father, many, many times. I have hidden things that I thought was for the benefit of others. I am deeply sorry."

"Marie, you have confessed these sins time and time again. God knows you are sorry and forgives you."

"But I want to make my last confession before I pass this earth."

"Say a rosary, Marie. I give you absolution." The priest made the sign of the cross over Marie.

"May I receive the Blessed Sacrament?"

"Yes, Marie. I have brought the Holy Eucharist for you." He reverently placed the consecrated host upon her tongue. "And now I anoint you." As he anointed her eyes, ears, nostrils, lips, hands, and feet with oil, he prayed, "Through this holy anointing and by His most tender mercy, may the Lord pardon you whatever transgressions you have committed by sight, hearing, or speech."

"I feel ready now, Father, for my maker to take me."

"He will receive you in all your grace and in all your splendor since you have lived your life for others and in God's name."

"Thank you, Father. Will you call my daughter, Philomene, in now? I want to spend the time I have left with her. She is such a blessing in my life."

"Of course, madame. May God be with you."

Marie lived for three more days with Philomene and her grandchildren at her side. She was able to talk to her daughter and grandchildren of many things—things they had never heard her speak of before. She told them of her first love, Jedidiah, and her first daughter, Felicity. She told of the Quadroon Ball that her mother forced her to attend.

"Oh, Mama, was it splendid? Did you waltz the evening away?" Philomene asked.

"I didn't notice that it was splendid. I resented having to be there to put myself on display for white men to ogle me and decide if they wanted me for a mistress. I only danced with one man who was over twice my age, and I quickly discouraged him to want me."

"How did you do that, Mama?"

"I told him my mama had to live with us and sleep with me and that she was very sick and vomited every night." Marie winked at Philomene.

"Oh, Mama. You think of the oddest things on the spur of the moment. I've seen you do that."

"Yes, my quick wit comes in handy. I left that ball before I had to endure another old man, thinking he could have me. Those Quadroon Balls are a thing of the past now, thank goodness."

She told of her love for her quadroon father. And she told of her best friend, Father Antoine, and how tolerant he was of the placees and their children. She told of the Ursuline nuns who taught her the Commandments and her catechism lessons.

When she tired, she would nap and then wake up, wanting to talk to her family. "Philomene, call Fidelia and Alexandre and Noemie to my boudoir. I want to talk to them again."

"I am here, Grandmama. It is me, Fidelia."

"My dear Fidelia. Did I ever tell you how I first met your grandpapa?"

"No, grandmama. I would love to hear."

"He lived next door to me on Bayou Road. On my way to work in the morning, I would see him sporting his full dress army uniform. It would stop my heart every time I saw him. He was such a handsome man. And he would greet me in the most fashionable way, tipping his hat to me. And he would pay me a call, asking if he could be of service to me. And if he saw me at Congo Square on a Sunday afternoon, he would walk me home to this house."

"Oh, I wish I could have known him."

"Alexandre, are you here?" Marie asked, as she peered down to the foot of her bed.

"Yes, Grandmama. Dear Grandmama, did you know your own grandmama?"

"Yes, I did. My grandmama, Catherine Henry, was a marchande. She worked very hard selling callas and foodstuffs on the streets and in the French Market. The *Les Vendeuses* supported their families with their businesses. My grandmama bought this very house we live in. And she always brought us food."

"I thank her for all the prosperity she has brought to this family through her hard work," Alexandre said.

"Noemie, is that you, my youngest?"

"Yes, Grandmama."

"Come here, my youngest. Let me see you closer. I want to have a moment to admire you," Marie said.

Noemie walked next to Marie's bed and bent to kiss her cheek. "I love you grandmamma."

"I feel such peace," Marie said. "And beauty all around me. I love you, my children. I feel God in the room."

Marie closed her eyes, and went into a deep sleep, and never opened them.